Falling Over

weird fiction by
JAMES EVERINGTON

infinity plus

Copyright © 2013 James Everington

Cover image © geniebird
Cover design © Keith Brooke

All rights reserved.

Published by infinity plus
www.infinityplus.co.uk/books
Follow @ipebooks on Twitter

'Falling Over' first appeared in *Penny Dreadnought Volume Two: Descartes' Demon*
'Haunted' first appeared in *100 Horrors* from Crunetus Libri Press
'New Boy' first appeared on the *Dark River Press* website
'Drones' first appeared in *Sirens Call* issue 2
'A Dream About Robert Aickman' first appeared on the author's website

No portion of this book may be reproduced by any means, mechanical, electronic, or otherwise, without first obtaining the permission of the copyright holder.

The moral right of James Everington to be identified as the author of this work has been asserted by him in accordance with the Copyright, Designs and Patents Act of 1988.

ISBN-13: 978-1490339139
ISBN-10: 1490339132

BY THE SAME AUTHOR

The Other Room
The Shelter

CONTENTS

Falling Over 7
Fate, Destiny, and a Fat Man from Arkansas 37
Haunted 57
New Boy 59
The Time Of Their Lives 85
The Man Dogs Hated 113
Sick Leave 123
Drones 151
Public Interest Story 159
Epilogue: A Dream about Robert Aickman 191
Author Notes 193

More from infinity plus 199

FALLING OVER

Ever since Michelle has come back from hospital, I've not been sure that it's really her.

By this I don't mean that her personality has changed, that the shock of the fall has shaken her confidence, or left her tired and prone to staring into space (although both of these are in fact true); I literally mean that she went in but didn't come out; that something has taken her place.

Which shows, given that another part of me knows that it certainly *is* her, that it is my own sanity that I should be questioning, my own identity rather than that of the girl I've fancied all term.

I am looking at her now; looking at her reflection in the window at least, for I am facing away from her. Is she aware that I am looking? Michelle is sitting at the table in our communal kitchen area; another girl called Grace is making her a cup of tea, and giving her looks of half-concern, half-admiration (Grace has always been somewhat under Michelle's shadow). I am pretending to wash-up, half-heartedly scrubbing at the first plate from the stack, while studying Michelle's reflection. It is superimposed over a bleached English sky, making her look paler than she really is.

The halls of residence are disturbingly quiet, for we three are almost the only ones on this floor – it is the holidays and most of the students have gone home. For reasons I won't go into some of us have nowhere else to go, and so we stay. There is a becalmed atmosphere; any radios or TVs switched on seem too loud on their old settings. There are a few others scattered on the floors above us, but although we hear signs of their existence a certain lethargy prevents us from seeking them out. Instead we sit together in this kitchen (although during term-time we are hardly all best friends). The only other person on this floor is called Christophe; I don't know where Christophe is. Looking out the window at the lifeless campus I imagine we are lost at sea, everyone else having been saved but us. A plane silently crosses the sky, glinting in sunlight which doesn't reach us down here, but I make no attempt to wave for rescue. Behind me, the song on the radio cracks up with static, as if we really were adrift.

Michelle is dressed in jeans and a familiar baggy jumper that she always wears when there are no guys around whom she wants to impress. She says she knows it is too large but it is soft and comforting; it was a present from her sister. Her hair is tied back – she normally has a habit, Michelle, of playing with her hair, unconsciously twisting a lock around her fingers. In a completely characteristic gesture she raises her hand to do this, then lets it drop because her hair is back, all without noticing. She says something to Grace and her eyes do that thing of hers where she blinks in rapid succession, then focuses on you again as if seeing you for the first time. Despite her proclaimed tiredness her voice is as precise as always – she never 'umms' or 'ahs' but remains silent until she has figured out what to say. Which doesn't normally take her long. Her accent is somewhat plummy (which I find sexy, with her) although her background is similar to mine: nothing special.

I hear the noise of car motors, distant from a road I cannot see. They are coming home from work again, and I am so out of synch with their daily rhythm that I am surprised it is so late already. I only got up a few hours ago, and my day is yet to come.

Michelle does that thing with her eyes *again* as she thanks Grace for the tea, and Grace smiles back somewhat nervously. This interaction between the two of them is in keeping with everything I've seen previously; it isn't just Michelle's appearance and body-language that are manifestly the same as before, but everyone else's perception of her, their relationship to her. *So why do I think that it's not her?*

Maybe it is the bandage around her head like some kind of bandana. She doesn't need it, it is to hide stitches rather than to protect the wound or staunch bleeding. She doesn't want anyone to see the (five) stitches in her head – which is reasonable enough – more importantly it is *in character*. Nevertheless her bandage does make her look different, almost surreal: she looks like a disaster survivor, a terrorist victim interviewed on TV, while she sits at our table drinking tea and moaning about coursework (she is writing her final year dissertation on 'The Geo-Politics of Oil' or some-such and she has to revise it almost every news broadcast). The white bandage makes her face seem too pale, as if she hasn't recovered lost blood. It seems to shade into the skin of her forehead.

But I know, it isn't the bandage. I would still feel the same suspicion if it wasn't there, still have the same nagging feeling that she is an impostor, a chameleon, an impersonator. That I have no evidence to back up this theory (and indeed much that refutes it) doesn't make my feeling go away; it makes it stronger, it convinces me how clever she, it, is. I must be going mad, I must have read *Invasion Of The Bodysnatchers* one too many times. Except I have never read it, and this is no sci-fi: *it isn't her*.

"Hey," Michelle says to me. "You're very quiet. Aren't you glad I'm back?"

I look at the plane, not at her. I try to see it for what it is: 400 people sitting strapped in, reading, sleeping, talking, farting... But I can't keep that image in my head at the same time as watching the silver dart of the plane. Even its pollution looks otherworldly; beautiful.

But Michelle is still waiting for an answer. I mustn't let on that I suspect. After all, it was me that found her.

I was in Christophe's room at the time. The girls were elsewhere, watching some traffic camera TV show, so we had retreated to drink beer and listen to the radio – a neutral choice since neither of us liked each other's CDs. It was supposedly night outside, but the on-campus lighting made it hard to tell. Every fourth or fifth light had a CCTV camera fitted – a hangover from some campus crime-wave that had never really abated, just become the accepted norm. Christophe had left his curtains open, and so every so often you'd see one of those cameras rotate, an unnerving reminder of the human hand behind the lens. Or is it just software? It worries me, when you see them move; I know I would have more of a sense of humour if I was adjusted, rather than this itchy feeling of being watched.

We were talking, Christophe and I, about the *future*, a vague but compulsive topic that has much occupied the paranoid parts of my mind recently. After all, there are just over two terms left, and then this degree course that I took as a stopgap (not knowing what else to do with my life) will be over. Barring catastrophe, I will achieve an honourable result in a course that leaves me fit for no job, except to teach similar courses. Of course, the lecturers would argue that *employability* is not the be all and end all of knowledge, and I would agree. But I *still* have no idea what to do with my life, and this thought makes me feel both desperate and apathetic – looking ahead, my life just disappears into a black-hole in nine months time, unknown and unobservable to anyone outside the periphery, including myself.

Christophe however, has it all sorted out. Or rather, his dad has – Christophe's father is high-up in some faceless corporation, one whose actions would no doubt be stained and corrupt with oil, if I could be bothered to look them up. And so Christophe has all the money he needs – he is a student but he has savings; he has *shares* for fuck's sake. He already has contacts among his dad's friends in the city, which will guarantee him a foot on the rung of a very tall ladder when he graduates. So Christophe doesn't want to talk about the future, or its attendant worries in my mind. Christophe wants to talk about girls.

"You know Grace likes you," he says, opening another beer.

"Fuck does she," I say. "She *likes* Michelle." Christophe laughs because it's true, sometimes the way Grace admires Michelle borders on infatuation: the way she follows her around, copies what she does, always harmonizes... But I doubt she actually fancies her.

Does she fancy me? It would be typical if she does – since the holidays started we have all been spending too much time together in these deserted halls, isolated by their perceived emptiness and the grey winter outside (I have started to feel an odd *unease* stepping outside, a sense of vague uncertainty and lack of purpose. It is cold out there, but not as cold as it should be this time of year). And in our isolation we have played out our little micro-dramas of lust in different combinations: I want to sleep with Michelle; Christophe wanted to sleep with Michelle and then wanted to sleep with Grace; Grace wants to sleep with Michelle (maybe) *and* me. God knows who Michelle wants to sleep with.

"Seriously," Christophe says, still on about the Grace thing.

"She isn't my type," I say, and she isn't – not because of the way she looks or the way she is, but because the one clear idea I have of my future is that I want Michelle to be in it. Never mind that the Michelle-future is a pipedream, whereas a Grace-future might just possibly work out. I want Michelle in the same way I want things from the brightest, gaudiest adverts. "What's

Michelle going to do when she finishes?" I ask. "Has she said anything to you?"

"Nope – she's a loser too," Christophe says. Once Christophe has put you into one of his little mental boxes there is no easy way out, and I am frightened by the fact that he will no doubt attain a position of real power in this country, and yet he barely seems to know he's born. He imagines he is slumming it with us sometimes, I feel, treating us as equals when at best we will be employees of people like him in the next world. It's like an unconscious caste system in his head. But one that others share, and maybe they are right and maybe I am a loser, for I have yet to summon the energy to even go and see the university careers adviser. I have yet to work out what I would actually say.

Upstairs on the floor above us there is the sound of movement – other stowaways on this abandoned ship of ours. The radio takes a break from music for a brief, rushed news bulletin – the presenter sounds like she just wants to rattle through the headlines as quickly as possible (and admittedly they would be scary if you stopped to think about them). Only the traffic report is lingered over – all gridlock and overturned chemical lorries.

"Bloody fucking hippies," Christophe says, apropos of an environmental protest march that is alleged to be blocking traffic. "Talk about shutting the door after the horse has bolted!" Do I have the right to feel angry with him when I am not there; have not contributed?

I get up to go to the bathroom. I'm halfway down the corridor when I hear a faint sound, almost a tapping sound. It is on the other side of the door that leads to the stairwells to the other floors. It gives me pause, for it doesn't sound like one of the girls – when you live with people for awhile you can identify them by the sounds of their footsteps or whatever, but this sound is different. Is it the sound of something moving, something alive... is it trying to keep quiet?

Somewhat nervously I open the door and Michelle falls through. She had obviously been sprawled against it, at the bottom of the stairs; the sound I heard was her fingers scratching against the wood. There is blood spreading down her face from a wound to her head – so much of it and so bright that it looks like a bad special-effect to me, not something I am inclined to believe in. Her eyes are closed; I can see her lips moving. For a moment the shock is so great that I almost fall myself.

She has obviously fallen down the stairs, and I completely ignore all the advice they give you about people whose back might be broken – I try to move her, cradling her and lifting her up so that she is half-sitting, half-leaning against me. She is half-awake, woozy.

Michelle's eyes flutter as they struggle to open; when they do she seems pleased to see me, in a vague sort of way – I can't help the thought that it would be like this if we woke up together some morning: the slow coming to consciousness, the hazy pleasure of recognition... But my cries have alerted the others and suddenly they are both here – Christophe is calmly calling for an ambulance on his mobile; Grace is just standing behind us, her face drained of what little colour it had. She is wringing her hands like it is her fault, like it has happened to her. But it is not Grace that I feel angry with but Christophe, for he is competently doing the things that I should have done.

Then Michelle's grip tightens on me and I panic for a second, for the way she is holding me is suddenly desperate, clingy. But she is just trying to pull herself up to speak to me. I try to calm her, to tell her whatever she wants to say can wait, but she is insistent. Her breath is hot against my ear as she whispers into it, her voice husky like a seduction...

But I couldn't tell what she said.

I couldn't work it out, and now I have the nagging feeling that I have missed something important. I am sure she was herself then, Michelle, for that moment at least, with the same conviction that I feel that the person drinking tea in our communal kitchen isn't someone I know. But she has just asked me if I am glad to have her back, and I say of course I am. I wish you'd never left, I say, and Michelle's reflection smiles, slightly confused.

I leave the kitchen and find Christophe in the communal TV room, which is of course deserted. The whole room is a throwback to last century – all students have TVs in their rooms now. The TV here looks old-fashioned, redundant technology. The colours look off; the ratios are all wrong. Christophe has a large TV and no end of gadgets in his room, but here he is sprawled out across the sofa, as if enjoying the perversity of being alone in such a large room. He is watching 24hr news, and from the empty beer cans by his feet I can tell he must have watched the same looped bulletins over and over, which can't be healthy. The sky framed in the window is darkening towards grey, and the planes are now only identifiable by their blinking lights.

I sit down next to him, practically on his legs until he reluctantly makes room. I know better than to ask for any of his beer.

"Listen," I say. "I need to talk to you. It's Michelle. Have you noticed..." I pull back on my words, on their insanity. How can I voice my concerns, when I know they must be ill-founded? But I need to tell someone, if only for them to laugh at me, to confirm I am a loon.

"It's Michelle," I say again, talking over the TV financials. "She's different... I mean she doesn't *look* different but she just is... different." I am aware that my words aren't quite satisfactory for what I have to express, but can find no others.

"Hallelujah," Christophe says. "It's about time." He looks bored, unconcerned, still watching TV. I am somewhat taken aback, for this isn't the reaction I expected.

"Huh?" I say. "You mean... You've noticed it too?"

"Course," he says, then swears as static cloaks the screen for a second. "Months ago."

Months ago – but that's not right, that is before she went to hospital; before she fell. I don't say this, but Christophe sees me looking at him.

"When I stopped fancying her!" he says loudly. "And now *you* don't fancy her either, because now there's you and Grace." He grins evilly. "Of course she seems different, now you're not blinded by her, after all these months, now you've got your head out of her arse."

"No, that's not it..."

But Christophe is half-drunk and insistent. He seems intent on the idea that me and Grace should get together. I realise it's pointless to continue to talk to him, but I need to bring the conversation back to some kind of normality before I can leave. So I ask him when *he* stopped fancying Michelle.

"Well I still...," he begins, blinking as if making an internal adjustment. "But she'll never *amount* to anything mate! Not with all her... views. Getting in the way." Just then his mobile rings, and I am glad. I don't know why I am angry – because Michelle was being criticised, or because I know he was levelling some of the same criticism at me. But he is wrong – my 'views', such as they are, seem flimsy and ill-founded, unable to guide me. They don't stop me buying things I don't need, just make me uneasy afterwards.

Christophe leaves the room to take his call – he takes a number of such calls, secretive, but not like he doesn't trust us.

Just like there are certain things that you don't talk about in front of children.

I sit and watch TV and try to relax. The beer has been left and now I help myself, gulping quickly even though it is better than the own-brand supermarket piss I am used to. I channel-hop but nothing on any of the stations suits my mood. After I have flipped round twice I feel somewhat numb. I make an effort to get up before I settle into an acceptance of something I don't even want to watch. It is night outside by now, but the sky still seems the wrong colour; just like the ones on this brute of a TV.

I still need to talk to someone – Grace it is then. I will just need to get her alone, away from Michelle... away from the thing that *isn't* Michelle I mean – I must remember to keep that distinction clear in my mind, or things will only get confusing. She still has that smile that sends tremors through me: the only sensations that have seemed unmediated recently. I must be wary, now that I know the truth about her, or recognise some of the lies at least.

I leave the TV room and see Christophe, quoting numbers into his mobile. He looks up at me and I realise if I go straight to find Grace he'll believe his little theories. So I pretend to head to my room instead; but Michelle finds me first.

"Thank Christ for that," she says. "I finally managed to shake her off." For a moment I have no idea who she means, not with the confusing distinction of two Michelles in mind – who has thrown off whom? But then I realise she means Grace, and I shrug sympathetically.

"Ever since I got back she's been *following* me," Michelle says. She unconsciously raise a hand to touch her bandage (like she used to with her hair).

"She means well," I say. "And she's lonely. I mean, not just lonely because everyone else has left. Proper lonely."

"I know but why me?" Michelle says. "Why do these people always fixate on me? I was thinking about this in hospital, and I decided I don't need it. Thinking about a lot of things actually. I figured some stuff out."

Her words unnerve me, perhaps because this little speech is the first time Michelle's double *hasn't* sounded like the real thing; the first time her words haven't tallied with my memories. She seems genuinely annoyed as she speaks and I imagine a vein underneath her bandage, pulsing, like something independently alive.

"Like what other things?" I say, thinking: the hospital was where it happened, so maybe that's where the clues lie. And I think, why didn't we go and *visit* her, why couldn't we escape these shipwrecked halls of residence even once, and go and see our friend in hospital? I have not thought this before, and I feel a chill, as if the conspiracy that I am caught up in is also one that I am unwittingly responsible for.

"Oh the future," Michelle says, "things people have said." Her tone is vague but the look on her face isn't – she stares me straight in the eye. Things *I* have said? What have *I* ever said?

Michelle reaches out and takes my hand.

And I look down and think: there was a tan-line on your finger before. All summer you wore that plastic toy ring that some boy won for you at the fair, some guy we never even met but was obviously important to you, because despite the fact that you tried to laugh off the ring as plastic kitsch, and pass off your wearing of it as ironic, you keep pushing it up your finger because you were afraid it might slip off. And then one day it was gone, and the tan you'd got from your days outside in the sun was in contrast to the white that remained underneath. And that tan-line *hadn't yet faded*, despite trips to the sun-bed when your student budget would allow it. But now when I look down at your hand it's not there, not just faded but gone, your skin one-tone. As if you had been created afresh. Created anew from the original design, minus any blemishes that occurred later...

But even as I am thinking all this, even as I realise this is the first real *proof* – physical evidence – that what is happening isn't all in my head – even as I am thinking this I am allowing Michelle to take my hand, and somewhat shyly lead me down the corridor to her room. She is still talking about some of the realisations she had in hospital after her blow to the head, but I am not listening because my heart is giddy. As Michelle fumbles the key one-handed into the lock, I look away and realise Grace is standing at the top of the corridor, watching us...

Grace, I think. I was on my way to find Grace. And not just because I wanted to explore my conspiracy with her, but because I am lonely; proper lonely. But Grace seems such a long way away at the other end of the corridor, and I am not sure which of us the look of accusation in her eyes is directed at anyway. She could just as well be mad with Michelle as me. My head is somewhat fuzzy from Christophe's beer, and Michelle is talking about the future to me, and *she* isn't even drunk (she isn't allowed alcohol because of the pills) and I look away from Grace and allow Michelle to lead me into her bedroom; allow this even as I look again at the hand that pulls mine again, and become convinced that this isn't Michelle at all, and that I might actually be in danger.

The next morning I awake in Michelle's bed, and she is asleep beside me. Our exertions in the night have caused a few faint specks of blood to stain her bandage from underneath, and I feel a moment's distaste.

The dawn outside is dull, but still manages to find its way through her cheap curtains, as does the noise of the rush-hour. I look to one side and on Michelle's bedside table there is a collection of Get Well cards that she has retrieved from hospital. I nudge them open with my fingers so that I can see the names inside – her parents; her sister; Christophe. So one of us did visit her in hospital after all. My paranoia finally catches on that I am awake and I remember; I look at Michelle but her hands are underneath the covers and I can't see the uninterrupted tone of her skin, the clear-cut evidence of the night before.

Grace, I think, I was on my way to find Grace and you distracted me. As if I not only believe in body-snatchers, but mind-readers too now.

I look again at the card from Christophe – what he has written inside is nothing beyond the usual clichés: *Get Well Soon* – yet I can imagine his voice dwelling on that *"well"*, implying we weren't just sick but lazy, feckless, losers. Later on in life people like Michelle and I will just be small pluses on Christophe's asset sheet (or someone very much like him). In abstract I hate people like Christophe; yet ever since everyone else left he has effectively been my best friend. It is like one of those TV documentaries where two diametrically opposed people are made to live with each other: the budding capitalist and the... what? Because our beliefs are not opposed at all, for I have no beliefs strong enough for anyone to oppose. I am just the soon to be ex-student, adrift.

But goddamn Christophe! Yesterday he claimed he didn't fancy her! Yet I know him well enough to know he doesn't invest without hope of return – he wouldn't have bought that card unless he liked her. Maybe that's why he's been so intent that Grace likes me. His comments to me were misdirection, moves in a game I didn't even know we were playing.

But if it was a game then I won didn't I? I got the girl. And she wasn't drunk and it won't be a one night stand. So fuck you

Christophe, with your sneering looks whenever I sketch out my ambitions. Because I got the girl – *whoever* she is.

I look at her again, at the bandage across her head. Dare I lift it up; would I wake her? What am I expecting to see but slowly healing stitches anyway? But although Michelle's face is the same as I remember I am overcome by a feeling of fakery at the sight of it, and I suddenly have to move, to get away from her.

"Where y'going?" Michelle mumbles, eyes still closed, as I hunt for my clothes.

"To get us some coffee!" I say brightly, and I feel the fakery in my own voice too, in the whole interaction.

Just then there is a bang at the door; Christophe shouting.

"Quickly," he says. "Grace is hurt."

I dash out into the corridor wearing just my boxer-shorts, while Michelle hurriedly dresses. The usually unflappable Christophe is looking fazed – every time he moves towards Grace she bats him away. Grace herself is standing in a beige dressing gown, which is stained with blood. I cannot see the source; she has blood on her hands and keeps rubbing them against the material of her dressing gown. Guiltily, I half-expect her to turn her hands wrist upwards and for me to see twin cuts there, one for Michelle and one for me, after Grace saw us together last night. That is why she is repeatedly beating Christophe's attempts at help away – not because she wants to die, but because she wants Michelle to be here, for her to see as well as me.

But getting closer I see her wrists are fine; the blood is in fact coming from a cut to the scalp, and when she runs her hands through her hair she keeps bloodying them. Scalp wounds bleed a lot, so it probably isn't as serious as it looks – nevertheless Grace is very pale and obviously afraid. Her grey eyes fasten on mine and she pushes past Christophe towards me.

"I don't want to go to hospital," is the first thing she says.

"Stop being idiotic," Christophe says, "your head's bleeding!" He shakes his own head at me, then makes another attempt to put his arm around Grace's shoulders so that he can lead her down the corridor.

"I don't want to go to hospital!" Grace shouts this time, and twists away from him. I move in front of her, for Christophe's irritation obviously isn't helping. I try and hold her gaze and ask her what happened.

Her eyes flicker as if she were about to tell an untruth, or at least something of which she is uncertain. "I... I don't know what," she says, brow furrowed. "I was just walking and I... I was daydreaming I guess and I just... fell over. Like I was pushed but there was no one there."

Michelle is out of her room and hurrying towards us now; Christophe is telling her what happened.

"Don't let me go to the hospital," Grace says quietly, making it between me and her. "Not like Michelle..." I wipe blood from her forehead because I don't know what to say: although I know she needs stitches I am reluctant to tell her this. I should have spoken to her last night – has she had suspicions herself? Just because she was acting natural around Michelle doesn't mean she hadn't spotted anything; after all *I* tried to act natural too. Maybe we just fooled each other. But did we fool Michelle? I don't know and now Michelle is here, hugging Grace, asking me if anybody has called a taxi. I take the opportunity to check her hand again, and the ring-line has definitely vanished. This is real enough, it isn't all in my head. Whatever *this* is, for I still have no idea what is going on.

Grace repeats her request not to go to hospital, now that Michelle is here.

"Of course you've got to go," Michelle says, all business, like a mother ignoring her child's heartfelt fears of the darkness. "Don't you agree?" she says to me, to get me to back her up.

Grace looks at me and there is a plea in her eyes, but much as I see that pleading I also see the blood that isn't stopping, dark red on her scalp. "You need to go," I say.

"Will you come with me?" she says directly at me.

"Sure," I say, "we'll go in the taxi together..."

"I've got a car," Christophe says.

I look up in some astonishment. "What?"

"Where the hell do you think I've been trying to lead her for the past ten minutes?" Christophe says, in the voice of one announcing the first checks of a forced mate.

"Since when did you have a car?" I'm angry because I can feel him taking over again, feel my own adulthood diminish next to his. I can't even drive, another misalignment with the real-world that Christophe mocks. But he has never mentioned owning a car before – not that I am surprised. "Did Daddy buy it for you?" I add, before I've even given him chance to reply to my first question.

"Is this really the time?" Michelle snaps. "We need to get her to A&E, a taxi could be ages, not that you've even ordered one." She is angry at me, at my inefficiencies.

"I'll get dressed," I say, straightening up, suddenly feeling cold and self-conscious in just my underwear. But I am miles from my own room; I could just get yesterday's clothes from Michelle's but even then...

"There's no time!" Christophe and Michelle say in unison, and their synchrony shocks me for a second. "Should have slept in your own room last night," Christophe says with an evil look at me, and instead of being annoyed at him, Michelle just smiles.

"She wanted me to go with her," I say, as the two of them take hold of Grace, one either side of her gripping her elbows, hauling her off like she really has done harm to herself. My words sound like a child's, plaintive sentiment ready to be ignored. Grace is struggling, but mutely, like she is half resigned to her fate. Like I have let her down too. I don't follow. Michelle glares at me over her shoulder, for not being any help, for creating complication where none exists, and I know it was a one-off last night after all – there's no future there. I have made an incorrect decision, and allowed myself to be judged by a girl whose standards I no longer even understand.

It's *not* Michelle remember, I tell myself, something has taken her place in hospital... and the thought of this doppelganger is now oddly comforting – the *real* Michelle wouldn't have rejected me... But I know the feeling of comfort is illusory, for there is danger here, and I doubt I'll ever see Grace again. Oh, something will come back, bandaged up and with scars I never found erased, but it won't be Grace. They will have gotten to her too.

After the three of them are out of sight, my sense of powerlessness fades. I need to find out what is going on. And in all the confusion with Grace, Michelle has left her room unlocked...

When I find it, it is almost too easy, like fake clues have been planted directly in my path – I find Michelle's diary. It is almost too obvious.

Everyone has gone home for the holidays except for me and a few others, I read. Michelle's handwriting is entirely legible, as if she'd wrote it out neat for the class. But despite this clarity there is an uncertainty to the content – although it is never written directly, each line seems to hint at the fact that girls like Michelle don't really keep such diaries anymore, in this late age. As though the sincerity of each sentence is contradicted by an irony affecting the whole. I skim read the latest entries, not really knowing what I am looking for. *Everyone seems to be sticking to their own floor – annoying because that boy I really like from lectures is on Floor 2 and I don't even know if he's still around. Last year he was so drunk I doubt he even* remembers *what we did together. So* bad *that I can't remember his name! Drunk too. Maybe I should go and look see if he is still around.*

Still feeling faint. Thank god I didn't go home – Mother would be *unbearable* if she knew. More unbearable, I mean.

......

Talked with others about plans after uni today. None of us know except C, who was being his usual self! Flattering that he likes me though, with his expensive tastes. G will end up being a teacher or nurse surely, she was only copying anxiety to fit in. World outside is going crazy too – keep the news switched off.

Floor 2 was empty when I went up – full of ghosts creaking. No sign of that boy!

......

Saw him today! Was shameless! He's practically all alone up there, and I said I was too down here. *Strongly* hinted that I could do with some company – talk about playing hard to get Michelle! Ah well. He's coming down tonight with some wine and DVDs.

Wish G would stop following me around, she better not turn up tonight! At least those boys have hormones as an excuse – decided they *both* fancy me now? Christ, it's this place, too empty – the mind makes shit up.

......

Fuck, fuck, fuck, *who* was that boy? Fuck!

......

No wait, calm down. The mind makes shit up, you said it yourself.

......

But shit wasn't he circumcised the first time?!!!

......

Michelle's handwriting had been getting steadily more ragged as I'd read, but for the next entry it was back to its previous neat and tidy progress across the page.

How drunk was I last night? (And how hung-over this morning – but then I've had this background headache for days.) Should tear the above pages out, I'm obviously stir crazy. But leave them. I can't help thinking...

I'll go up today, *sober*, and speak to Floor 2 boy again (still don't remember his name) and that will sort me out. That and aspirin. Stop craziness. Which I don't need. I need to *sort stuff out*, work out what graduate placements to apply for. Writing this knowing I won't. C has invited me to some careers fair, transparent, but it won't be because of that I don't go. I'll just end up kicking around here with the other two. We can all be losers together. Until the money runs out. Or the oil dries up and we all end up back in the caves anyway.

Better go upstairs and find that boy though, so I can get my head into some kind of working order. Before I lose my nerve.

The was the last entry, dated the day she fell over. After that, nothing. I wasn't expecting entries for the time she was actually in hospital, but I was for the days after. But it is like diary writing is a childish, teenage thing that she has suddenly grown out of.

But the Floor 2 boy – that is a clue surely? The boy who she went up to find on the day she fell. And the person I have read more about in Michelle's diary than myself, despite the fact she sees *me* every day, despite the fact that she doesn't even know *his* name...

Without letting myself think too much I drop Michelle's diary on her bed, leaving the clasps open. Let her guess that I read it, that I know her secrets... My head is pounding as I leave her room and head towards the stairwell. I am dizzy on the stairs, and scared I will fall myself. I hold tightly onto the banister, and I feel enflamed, tenacious despite my dizziness. I welcome the unexpected struggle of the climb, for without obstacles my anger would be a tantrum only; with them my fury seems justified... The fact that it is without cause doesn't signify, only its intensity.

Floor 2 is an identical layout of corridors and rooms to our own, and for a moment I have the feeling that the staircase I have climbed is like one from an Escher drawing, and I have returned to where I started from. The windows are so dirty you can't even get a feeling of height. Like our floor, Floor 2 is deserted, almost everyone elsewhere for the holidays. The corridors seem longer, as if emptiness isn't an absence but a physical thing, pushing at the boundaries. But the boy I am looking for was here at least up until last week, so there is an outside chance that I'll find him. There are a hundred doors, but I can hear faint music; I walk down the corridor slowly, quietly, a hunter following the trail of some hectic animal, for the music is loud, riotous yet synthetic, the rush of beats exactly the kind of thing I despise.

The music is coming from behind a closed door, and I pause in front of it. What exactly am I going to say; why have I followed this trail here? Because I believe that the room this dreadful music is coming from is the room of the boy from the diary? And furthermore that the boy is some kind of doppelganger (*shit wasn't he circumcised the first time*) who somehow caused Michelle to fall down the stairs and become a double in her turn? Every time I cross-examine my thoughts their ludicrousness seems obvious; yet I continue to think them.

Without knowing his name, how will I even check it's him? Could I recognise him from the fact that Michelle fancies him – has she a 'type'? Given the fact that she slept with me too, probably not. But that was an aberration, as she has made clear. And besides that wasn't *her*; the real Michelle slept with the boy behind this door. Twice.

But even that isn't true I think (still paused outside the door). For the second time Michelle slept with him (*shameless* I think, wondering what he did that was so special she came back) it wasn't who she thought it was but some bodysnatcher with original foreskin attached. So I am right to hate him – if I hit him hard enough, will I see the skin of his real face beneath?

Right too to be afraid.

Before I can knock or push open the door, it opens from the inside.

I start, flinch backwards. The person who opens it flinches back too. It obviously *isn't* the boy that Michelle liked.

"What the hell are you doing?" she asks.

Flustered, my mind tries to adjust from conspiracy plots to the more mundane and embarrassing fact that I have been caught snooping outside a girl's room.

"Your music...?" I improvise lamely. "Could you turn it down? I'm right below you, on the floor below..."

Some of the heat fades from the girl's face, although she still looks wary.

"Sorry," she says, cautiously apologetic and friendly. "I thought I was on my own; there's no one else up here you see."

"No one?" I say quickly, thinking of the boy I am after, but I realise I have said it *too* quickly, too eagerly, for the fright returns to the girl's eyes.

"No there are people," she says loudly, "there are other people here" – throwing her voice into a shout that echoes down the corridor, trying to make me believe she has someone to call for protection, if I try anything funny. As if anyone could hear her over the music.

"Wait I just meant are there any *blokes* up here?" I say, but she is already shutting the door, and my words don't make her stop, for if I was thing she feared I might have said that too. I make a grab for the door, but just manage to get my fingers nipped as it slams shut.

"Get away you freak or I'll call the police!" she shouts from behind the door, her fright obvious now. I turn and run, feeling out of synch with this situation I have somehow got myself into. Like one of those films where the good guys and bad guys are not who they first appear to be, and your brain lags as you work it out. Will she call the police? Even if she does, why am I running, for I would merely have to explain things to them and they'll see I've done nothing wrong. There's no crime but I am running as if guilty, hurtling downstairs so quickly that I almost trip, back to my floor, my room. I shut the door but don't put any music or TV on – I pace but try to keep quiet. I think of the campus security cameras outside, and shut the curtains.

If the body-snatchers get you, I wonder, do you even realise? But I don't understand what that thought even means.

I can't sleep, for the airplanes seem too low overhead, and the light coming through the windows seems unnatural.

The next morning I try and call Grace to see how she is, to see if she went under at the hospital. She'll be alright, I think, she'll be safe as long as she's not been anaesthetized. I have nothing to base this on, but cling to it with an odd certainty. But my mobile has no signal – I am sure it is a network problem, but it is hard not to think that the fault is deliberate, local, centred on me. I head towards the front of the halls of residence where there are some payphones, but they have no dial tones and my coins just clatter through the mechanism and fall out the other end. *This* I am not surprised by, this doesn't become a factor in my emergent paranoia, for the payphones are dilapidated relics of the days when mobiles were for the likes of Christophe only; I've never seen anyone actually use them. They have been superseded by later technology that can't be relied on.

I decide that I'll have to go to the hospital to find Grace – and I am surprised to find that my decision is not just based on the still unspoken fears clenched in my gut, but also on something Christophe said: *she likes me*. Assuming for one minute Michelle is Michelle and my delusions are proven just that – still, why was I so fixated on Michelle? I suddenly can't remember why.

I force myself outside, but after days of being confined to halls the outdoors just seems a continuation – the holidays have thrown up a localised fog which makes me feel enclosed in a vague bubble, my sight limited to its circumference. I walk down the path from our campus, past the Job Centre which is outside the exit – a nice irony that is not lost on those of us doing humanities degrees – and towards the main road. Strangers coming the opposite way through the fog loom up so quickly that I couldn't make eye contact even if I wanted to. The world appears in gasps and snatches through the mist. They are queuing round the block for petrol again, for fear of another price hike; their idling fumes add to the mist. My progress up the street is faster than that achieved by the rush-hour traffic, and I sense their antagonised looks as I pass: fuckin' student; fuckin' *pedestrian*.

There is no bus in sight yet and so I decide to walk to the 24hr garage (the one the cars are slowly working towards) to buy some chocolates or flowers for Grace. I feel even more self-conscious inside: the only person not buying war-inflated petrol. I quickly buy some chocolates, because the only flowers look plastic to me, even though they are promoted as real. Outside two motorists almost crash, going for the same pumps. Their tempers are up before they are even out their cars, their firsts clenched before they can even see each other properly in the mist. They curse at each other, but it doesn't quite come to blows.

One day, my son, all this will be yours.

A bus has somehow fought its way up the car clogged bus-lane, and I run to the stop. The bus is full of people studiously avoiding the world on the other side of the windows: plugged into headphones or bent over beach-fiction. It's only a local bus but they have the practised look of long-distance travellers, of people who have given up hoping their journey will arrive on time, and are concentrating on making the best of being there – I settle myself in too, but I am not the same as them, for I am surely the only one not riding to work. The idea and desire that one day I will be feels oddly remote, like an advert for something that you can't possibly imagine ever being able to afford.

The hospital is another building of identical corridors, painted with seemingly the same colours as my own halls of residence, lit by the same dusty strip-lights. There is an extravagant shop on the ground floor, where you can buy flowers, books, cuddly toys; but otherwise the place appears shabby and out of date. Nevertheless the receptionist I speak to is friendly and smiles at the box of chocolates I am clutching – she thinks I am some considerate boyfriend. But what boyfriend goes to hospital worrying that his girl might be someone else entirely? Worrying that the ring-line will have faded from her fingers? But I am getting muddled here, and anyway *I* didn't win Michelle that ring.

I find out from the friendly receptionist that Grace had been kept in overnight only as a precaution, because it was a head wound, and that she only needed a couple of stitches. There doesn't seem to be any concussion, she says, but you can never assume.

When I find Grace she seems very surprised to see me, and I can't stop myself from grinning. Because it is *her* – the certainty, the authenticity of her is so strong that it clarifies all my fears and feelings about Michelle. The mind makes shit up yes, but as I sit besides Grace and give her the chocolates I know it isn't making this up; and not my doubts about Michelle either (although I am not so certain if my doubts are any longer about her identity, or merely my own feelings towards her). Grace looks her usual self, with no bandages around her head; her stitches are faint and lost beneath her thick hair.

We talk for hours, Grace and I, and although I sense she is hurt and wary because of the way I went off with Michelle the other night, she doesn't mention it, and of course neither do I. In fact Michelle and Christophe aren't mentioned once, despite the fact that we have spent all our time with them these last few weeks, cut adrift in that pokey halls of residence. Nor do my body-snatcher theories get a mention; nor do they seem important. Instead we have the conversation we should have had the night before, the getting-to-know-you conversation. Not small talk, not the forced mini-biographies of those meeting for the first time, but a conversation that manages to be both relaxed and shy at the same time, a conversation where the embarrassment of revealing your real fears is balanced by the easy acceptance of them at the other end.

She wants to go travelling, Grace. Not just being a tourist (which she can't afford) but maybe doing some relief-work too. She says maybe she doesn't want to go alone. I ask her *why* she wants to go.

"Because the alternatives...," she pauses, looks away. "Everyone *knows* the world's got to change, but everyone just carries on as normal..." She shrugs and tries to make her tone light again. "Besides, it's a stop-gap if nothing else." And I know what she means – so what if it's a stop-gap? Why should your life be fixed and decided by twenty-one? There is no mention in our talk of us becoming a couple, and I realise I have yet to prove myself, after I basically slept with her friend. And besides that I am not blind to the practicalities – once the student loans run out neither of us really know what we'll be doing where – the travelling is a pipe-dream that hasn't been planned for yet. Nevertheless I feel happier and more purposeful that I have done for months. Maybe if *we* do things different, other things could change too.

About halfway through visiting hours, Michelle and Christophe turn up.

They have bought lavish presents from the hospital shop downstairs, and their obvious expensiveness makes my chocolates look cheap, unthoughtful. The two of them are smiling secret little smiles, and I wonder if they were holding hands before the moment they came in here. Michelle is wearing a bandage around her wound, still hiding something that I am no longer interested in. Grace's manner is polite yet distant with them, like with people you are told are your relatives, but whom you've never met before. I'm not sure whether this bothers them, or whether it's my imagination.

"Grace," Michelle eventually says, " do you mind if we have a moment alone?" – meaning me and her. "Christophe can stay here with you?" I look at Grace and our eyes meet; I see a little mental shrug in her glance – what harm can it do? We have reached an understanding, and as long as I am the person she thinks I am, neither Michelle nor Christophe can do anything about it (and if I'm *not*, why should she care?).

"Sure," Grace says. "Knock yourselves out."

I walk with Michelle back down the corridors, both of us silent. I don't think her silence is any kind of ruse though, for she seems genuinely tense, building up to something. In the meantime I am content to keep walking, to keep quiet. She is wearing a ring again I notice – is that to hide the evidence, the mysterious vanishing of the tan-line? Has this body-snatcher read my mind, is it trying to disguise... – but these thoughts seem false, appended to my consciousness, unimportant. There's no such thing as doppelgangers, no conspiracy – it was all part of the cracked and solipsistic paranoia I'd allowed myself to fall into because I was lonely... proper lonely. But now is the first time for months I've walked alongside Michelle (whoever she is) and not felt my centre of gravity slip. She has no power over me anymore, and this walk is a temporary pause in the conversation Grace and I were having. Whatever Christophe is doing or saying back in the ward doesn't signify either.

We have actually left the hospital, and are walking around the grounds in the fog. Michelle tugs at the collar of her long coat.

"You know I still keep dressing for winter," she says, "even though I know we'll never have ones as cold as we used to again."

I keep quiet, although I am warm myself. Above us, there is the noise of a plane, but the sight of it is lost in the fog-like clouds. Grace and me, I think vaguely; but something about the idea of us on that plane, youthfully saving the planet while leaving a trail of pollution behind us, suddenly strikes a false chord in my thoughts. Have I merely fallen for another fantasy?

"Have you decided what you're going to do after university?" Michelle asks, looking at me. Something lurks in her polite tone, implying she knows my sudden plans, and that they will come to nothing. I am overcome with a sudden repulsion at her presence – *why* have I not questioned, even in my own head, the fact that she is *still* wearing that bandage? That she has put on any old ring to hide that vanished tan-line? It is all I can do not to flinch, to keep walking at a steady pace while my mind is racing: my thoughts become clearer in the fog, the realisation that potential happiness with Grace is no protection against this predatory thing that walks besides me, and is again going through the motions of flirting: doing that thing of hers with her eyes which she knows makes me want her. That works.

Ahead of us I notice a solitary figure walking in the mist, in the same direction as us. I decide if I look at Michelle I might get angry, or worse get muddled again, and so I focus on that figure in front of me. He is going at the same pace as us, so we don't get any closer.

Out of the corner of my eyes I see Michelle smile to herself. "You see I'm wearing your ring again?" she says.

I *do* look at her now, in surprise, for the blunder she has made is so glaring: *I* never won that ring for her from the fair did I? And the one she is wearing isn't even the *same* one... What is she trying to convince me of; can this thing that I thought could read minds really have made such an error? And if so why is Michelle's face still smiling?

"What?" is all I say aloud, trying to keep the tone of my voice absent.

"The ring that you won for me at the fair?" Michelle says quietly. "Don't you remember?"

No, I think, there's nothing for me to remember. It was that boy, the one we never even met... I merely wanted to have won it for you, and wanting isn't good enough.

"Ummm?" I say, politely disinterested. We have paused and the figure in front of us has paused too, like it wants to keep an equidistance. I'm not even clear if it's male or female, can determine neither age nor race in this fog, which has only thickened as the sun has risen. The figure is so obscured I can't even make out its height properly; it shifts form in the mist like it is still waiting to adopt one permanently. I start walking again and Michelle follows me. The lonely figure starts walking again too.

"Don't you remember?" Michelle repeats, and for a moment the hurt in her voice sounds natural enough for me to consider it, but it can't be true, no matter *how much* I wanted it to be; I build conspiracy upon conspiracy; I imagine that all these months another has been walking around with my face, never in a room at the same time as me, but messing up my life.

The mind makes shit up, I think. If the body-snatchers get you, do you even realise? The deja-vu, the fact that I have thought these things before, makes my thoughts oddly automatic, as if learnt by rote.

I look at Michelle and suddenly realise *why* she is smiling, just why she is trying to take me in with lies that I will blatantly see through. It is because she doesn't have to try; I am already caught. She is just playing with me, giving me convincing proof that she lies, knowing that I will still end up suckered anyway. Already, Grace seems too far away to influence my actions. Maybe, if I had stronger convictions, they would have had to work harder, maybe then they would have made the effort to make their lies believable, to dig out the right ring, the real one that I (wanted) to have given her. But as is, they believe I am caught anyway; as soon as I realise what the trap is it will snap shut.

No, I think, all you have to do is keep walking until you get back to Grace, *and not to look at this Michelle besides you.*

Just then the figure in front of us starts to fall over.

It is like he has been shot (I can suddenly see it is a he), shot or put to sleep, it is that sudden: the way his head lurches, his whole body lurches to one side like someone has pushed him. And as he is pushed right his legs start to go beneath him, buckle, as if they are made of inappropriate materials with which to support him. It all seems to happen in slow motion, like it has been filmed and is being played at the wrong speed in front of us. The boy (who now looks like some student) falls so slowly that I manage to break into a run to get to him. I lurch arms outstretched, clumsy and off balance across the car-park tarmac towards him. But the fog thickens not lessens as I near him, or maybe it is all in my eyes, for my feet go suddenly as I am rushing forwards, I am off balance and off gravity, and I realise that the boy I saw falling has become more and more like myself as I've approached; his flesh has copied mine, he is me, my double, and we are falling over.

(And somewhere, I hear a girl cry out.)

I was knocked unconscious when I fell over, but Michelle got me to help – not far, since we were already at the hospital! We laugh. I have the same number of stitches in my head as her, although my bandage stretches the other way. She and Christophe came to see me every day at hospital – my fall was the worst so far, and so I am kept in for observation for awhile. I am not bothered that they always come together, for Michelle wears my ring, the one we shall say I won at the fair for her. And Christophe does not seem angry to have lost either, at least not as far as I can tell, for he has offered to put me in touch with some friends of his father, who work in the city.

Only Grace gives me funny looks.

She only comes to visit occasionally, and our conversations are briefer and more stilted each time. I have outgrown her, I suppose, for I have been thinking a lot alone in this hospital bed. She is so idealistic; so naive!

But she is right to be wary.

For there are so many of us now. I close my eyes, and hear the rush hour.

Right too to be afraid.

So many!

FATE, DESTINY, AND A FAT MAN FROM ARKANSAS

In his dreams, he saw the car from outside.

It was a white car, climbing up the exit from a flyover, going the wrong way. It was doing well over the speed limit but the oncoming traffic managed to avoid it. The car's white paintwork was speckled with both grime and the blood from the two pedestrians it had hit thirty seconds earlier. It reached the highest point of the flyover; below it other roads writhed in thick tangles. The road was clear of traffic ahead. But, as if not to be denied its chance for the spectacular, the car swerved violently and deliberately to the left, into the crash barrier. Which failed to hold. The car shot over the edge of the flyover, for a few seconds following the same trajectory in mid-air as it had held on the road. In those final seconds the driver turned and looked, not at his friend in the back, but at the smiling face and blank glasses of the fat man from Arkansas in the passenger seat... Then the car hit the ground bonnet first, with such force that the deaths inside should have been mercifully quick.

In his dreams he saw the car from outside, and himself, clamped and terrified in the driver's seat.

Tom awoke from his uncomfortable sleep, stretching and yawning. Normally, his dreams faded quickly when he woke, as if recognising the daylight; but this one refused to fade. He sat up on the back seat where he had slept, and looked for a while at the scenery blurring past his window with a worried frown on his otherwise baby-smooth features. Then he leaned forward and tapped the driver of the car on the shoulder.

Sean flinched at the contact, although he tried to pretend that he hadn't. He turned round and glared at his companion. They were both young men, in their mid-twenties, although Sean was two years older. Tom wished Sean would look at the *road*, rather than back at him.

"I had that dream again."

"What dream?" Sean said irritably.

"You know, the one I told you about. The one I had *before*. The one about the car crash and... and the fat guy."

"Oh *that* dream," Sean said, as if they always talked of dreams and he'd grown confused about which one. "It's only a dream." They entered a small village where a sign politely asked them to drive carefully. "Besides, you just imagined the fat guy," Sean said. Outside he saw a church, a bowling green, a family owned butcher – the village they were passing through was like some Tory wet-dream of England, and the two inner-city lads felt taunted and threatened by its presence, its smug air of permanence and durability. They could break into the large homes, but the insurance would pay; they could swear at the residents, and just reinforce their prejudices. Sean accelerated, felt some satisfaction as the white car sped past the bus stop. But there was no one standing there to tut disapprovingly – everyone was probably too rich to need the bus here, Sean thought angrily. The service had probably been stopped years ago. Leaving the small village, a sign thanked them for driving carefully, and although he hadn't this made Sean angrier still. He tried to calm himself – after all, he did *want* to drive carefully so as to not attract unwelcome attention, given that the boot was full of stolen goods... Yet his nervous irritation remained, like the fumes of a fuel that should've long since run dry.

Tom was also wondering why Sean was so worked up. He had known Sean for years, since he'd been twelve and Sean fourteen. Tom didn't tend to think about things too much, but he had semi-conscious and nagging doubts about why Sean had *ever* wanted to be his friend. He knew the fact that he was younger could no longer be used as an excuse for his deference, for the fact that Sean thought up the ideas, whereas he just tagged along, like hired help. Knew too that he reverted back to earlier childishness and excitability when he was alongside Sean, despite the fact that Sean professed to be angered by this. But he was glad Sean had stuck by him; without Sean he'd never have dared attempt anything as audacious as the robbery last night; even with Sean they'd almost blown it... But there was no point in thinking about that, for it was okay now, and they were on their way down to London. There weren't many fences where they came from who could give them a fair deal on the loot in the back of the car: the ornaments of precious metal, the grotty books and other religious paraphernalia. The designs on them were... unique. So Tom hoped, anyway. If it was worth as much as they thought then neither of them would ever need to return to the sink estate on which they'd both grown up.

The pair drove in silence for a while, neither able to think of anything to say. Occasionally they saw a police car and the silence grew tense and rigid, but the law didn't seem interested in them. It seemed too easy. When Sean did eventually speak he sounded uncomfortable, as though the two had only just met.

"It feels like winning the lottery, huh?"

"Uh huh," Tom agreed. "Yep." He wished Sean wouldn't look over his shoulder to speak to him; he wished it was his turn to drive. Although they were only going thirty miles an hour, if he closed his eyes and focussed Tom sensed how unnaturally fast that actually was, as if the surrounding car didn't exist, and he was travelling at that speed unprotected, the air whipping past his face... He felt doubly out of control, not driving and also confined to the back seat, like a child. But then where else was he supposed to sleep? They'd both been tired after the robbery, after their midnight dash.

"It's like something out of a movie, huh? All this stuff? I mean we normally steal phones and you know... TVs and stuff. Not these, these *chalices* and things. Not old Bibles."

"They're not Bibles," Tom said.

"Well, you know... religious books. I mean, not a real religion but ... Well it is to *them* I guess. The people who go there."

"Doesn't make it a religion" Tom said, and Sean didn't argue. Neither of them knew what they were talking about, after all. Tom never did, but Sean guessed he was right on this occasion – it wasn't a real religion, just a load of sad, sick fuckers, and stealing from them wasn't like stealing from a church, but in its way almost a *good* deed... – Sean wasn't trying to reason himself out of a sense of guilt, but one of fear.

They pulled into a service station, to fill up with petrol and take a hurried look around the mini-mart. Sean bought *The Mirror*, a scotch egg, forty Bensons, and a copy of *Razzle* which he slid inside his newspaper as he walked back to the car. Tom bought *Playboy*, some Smarties, and a *Ren & Stimpy* comic, which he slipped inside his magazine on his way back to the car. Outside on the forecourt he could hear the speed of the traffic rushing past; *if I just ran out into the road...* he thought; then shook his head as if his thoughts were physical distractions like flies. He'd had such feelings since he'd woken, not serious ideas but almost dream-like, creeping across his consciousness before he realised how silly they were. They must have been caused by his troubled sleep on the back-seat of a speeding car, by his nerves.

Tom got into the front seat; it was his turn to drive. The idea that some of the nervousness he was feeling would fade when he was in the driving seat proved false, for he still felt the same lack of control as he pulled out into the road, the speeding traffic swerving to one side of him. Just because he was driving, what control did he have? He could be the most careful driver on the road, but his fate could still be sealed by the mental calculations of the person coming up behind him who was talking on his mobile phone... *Slow down*, Tom said in his head; s*low down!* The car didn't decelerate, but moved into the other lane at the last moment, the driver still oblivious on his mobile as he passed. Tom's eyes flicked to the mirror, saw the other cars racing to catch him up.

Sean stretched out on the back seat, and idly flicked through the dull and clichéd pornography before tossing it aside, not feeling in the least bit aroused. He closed his eyes and tried to sleep – despite the pretence he had made last time Tom had driven, Sean hadn't slept at all since the robbery. This time though, his eyes felt heavy and he thought if he could just relax then he might be able to drop off. He felt the car jerk violently; heard Tom press the horn and swear, his voice stressed – Sean smiled: Tom was always a nervous driver. For a long time Sean lay with his eyes closed, worrying about the police, the reliability of their fence, and an American voice promising revenge in a just so tone: this is how things *will* be. And then he slept. And dreamt.

Neither of them wanted the grotesquely fat man to get into the car, but they both invited him to sit in the passenger seat. Which he did, cramming his buttocks into the tight space, barely managing to pull the seat-belt across his massive belly. Yet he neither grunted nor sweated nor struggled. Once he was in and the door was shut he told them, in an American accent, where to go. It was a little out of the way for them, and they were already late – but they did what he said. They drove south for a while, speeding up all the time. They were going roughly seventy miles an hour when they hit the teenage couple walking hand in hand across a pedestrian crossing. She turned and her face struggled with the split second comprehension of her death; he had been whispering into her ear and didn't even look round. The white car shook and jolted as it went across the bodies; a few drops splattered as high as the windscreen. The car didn't slow down, but accelerated towards the flyover. They both wished to act, even just to plead, but they just sat silent and immobile (the disconnected way his arms turned the wheel and his feet pressed the pedal didn't seem like any movement of his own). The fat man sat silent too, relaxed in the confinement of the seatbelt. The car climbed up the exit from the flyover, going the wrong way...

Sean awoke with a barely controlled noise of fear. Within seconds he was angry with Tom – the stupid little prick had got him all worked up with his talk of dreams: now he was having them too! Except that wasn't quite true. Sean hadn't managed to sleep the first time Tom had taken over the driving, but he had... dozed. His thoughts had wandered, with as little coherence and control as if he had been dreaming after all. And while he could remember no details, Tom's talk of car crashes and... and that fat guy had chimed perfectly with the vague feeling of dread he remembered, and which persisted.

"How long was I asleep?" he asked Tom. "This time?"

"About ten minutes. No, maybe fifteen."

Sean looked out the window, trying to keep a frown from his face. He was sure he'd heard that you had to sleep for at least an hour to go deep enough to dream. But then, he had been so tired... Sean felt even worse after his nap than before. He pulled out a cigarette, and rolled down the car window. There was nothing to look at in the scenery scrolling past, and his eyes defocused so that the sight became nothing but a rushed blur. He got bored, irritable, and flicked through his newspaper, saw the same usual load of shite: scandals, gossip, the low down on a boy-band apparently *'Destined For No 1!',* and a surprisingly accurate weather forecast.

"Hey, you wanna know your horoscope?" he asked Tom, more for something to say than through wanting to say it. Besides, he knew his friend liked hearing them, for Tom listened with childlike glee when they predicted great things.

"No, don't read them out," Tom said quietly. The car braked suddenly and Tom held down the horn; Sean was sprawled on the back seat and so didn't see what had happened.

"Aw come on, Taurus right?" Sean said. He started to read the bullshit about financial luck and a broadening of personal horizons due to travel, but Tom interrupted him:

"Just shut up will you! You're putting me off!"

Sean looked up from the paper – he couldn't see Tom's face, only his arm and hand on the gear stick. It was trembling.

"Well, fuck you too," he muttered, flinging the paper away in disgust that was half feigned to hide his confusion.

Tom stared out the window, aware of his friend's anger but unable to find anything to say to explain himself. Thought seemed hard, he was concentrating so much on driving – like he was a learner again, like it was a matter of life and death. Which he supposed it was. But the road didn't normally seem so wild, with traffic veering and swerving with no predictability, with invisible bumps in the road making the car judder and bolt, with unsignposted junctions, unexpected side-winds. He wanted to explain to Sean why he was so afraid, but he didn't know himself. He just knew that he was very scared and that the feeling had been getting stronger ever since the robbery. Of course he had been scared *during* the break-in as well, but that had been different, an adrenaline fuelled fear, alive with possibilities and so close to excitement it had made him feel high. Until he had seen the fat man: tall, but slumped under his own immense weight, leaning forward like a dinosaur, his head high and hairless, his spectacles glaring with reflected light, his teeth grinning horribly. He had introduced himself with an American accent, but Tom couldn't remember the odd sounding name. Then as Tom had stood there paralysed, caught red handed with the temple's goods in his pilferer's grip, the fat man had said he came from Arkansas but "long before it was called that." He had licked his fat round lips and then, smiling as if hungry, he had started saying the most horrible things... which Tom couldn't quite remember. He didn't want to. But now he felt like a rat in a maze, being prodded and electrocuted into going down certain routes...

It hadn't been a *real* temple. Just an old rented house, where people gathered. No one admitted to going, or to having friends who went; maybe friends of friends, maybe, but no one you personally knew... Nevertheless, people went – neighbours saw people entering at strange hours, and began to claim they heard chanting through adjoining walls. And of course, because no one knew anyone who went, the stories about what went on inside became spuriously specific and hysterical: animal sacrifice, child abuse. There were, apparently, strange relics and old, old books inside the house, books that told of old beliefs that should've been long since buried... No one knew who owned the house, it had been empty for years. Overnight it became daubed with lurid anti-immigrant graffiti – but still people came and went at odd hours, and any slight noise on the wind was claimed to chanting from its interior.

Some local kids disappeared, and while there was no actual connection that could be made to the 'temple', the locals found it hard not to make a connection in their minds. But still, it had been just a *house*, with no alarm and with no one in it after nightfall. Best of all, due to the resentment it had caused in the community the local police weren't going to care if it was broken into. They weren't going to investigate too hard. It had almost seemed *too* easy. Even the question of where to sell 'religious' artefacts in an almost godless (and penniless) estate had been answered within a couple of days: bizarrely, unrealistically, someone's brother worked in a museum in London and was known to pilfer things from the backrooms when they weren't on public display. So he had the contacts; he gave them the name of a fence. In the pub that night, Sean and Tom had agreed to give it a go – they would break in, steal what they could, and head straight down to London to meet the fence. It would be a long, long drive and they would have to take shifts; but an easy drive at that, for the route was basically a straight line south, and the navigation needed was minimal.

They were coming into the outskirts of the outskirts of London now, and the traffic had slowed due to the rain that had come lashing in sideways, allowing Tom to relax somewhat at the slower pace, despite the reduced visibility. His memory of the inside of the temple was fading, and he could forget somewhat that it was a real life place, which he had entered. Into which he had trespassed. He glanced around and saw Sean was asleep again, although his friend's sleep didn't look peaceful. Tom wondered if Sean was having the same kind of dreams he was, and what that would mean if it was true…

Tom cursed – he had just driven past the turning that they wanted, because he'd been so wrapped up in his paranoid daydreams. He considered waking Sean, but he decided that it wasn't anything to be worried by – there was bound to be another chance to make a right turn soon.

~

"Any chance of a lift?" the fat man said, and despite the raised last syllable (along with a thick eyebrow) it wasn't a question, not really. He tried to frame a negative reply, but his head was already nodding, dog-like and obedient. He felt his lips part and his mouth draw breath – his lungs swelled

and he knew he was about to speak; he had one last chance to refuse this but instead he heard himself say,

"Sure. Where're you going?" His friend in the driving seat said something similar. The American man smiled, his teeth somehow glinting despite the overcast day. His glasses were giant circles of reflected light across his flabby face. He told them where he wanted them to go. They both felt terrified, felt the urge to open the doors and bolt from the car – but the desire turned to nothing in their nerves, and they just sat there.

'That's where we're going," he heard himself saying, as if amazed by the coincidence of his desires and their destination.

"Yeah, get in!" his friend said, hands shaking and eyes terrified.

And the fat man did.

Sean awoke, having slept nearly twenty minutes this time. His back was aching from lying on the awkward back seat and his head felt fragile as well, as if he'd been drinking. Without getting up, he reached for and lit another cigarette, tossing his dead match to join its companions between the over exposed breasts of the *Razzle* centrefold, who was apparently called Rochelle. Sean felt he'd first seen Rochelle years ago, as if he'd been in the backseat of a car with her for a lifetime. For some reason he turned the page, but there she was again, in a grimly predictable pose. Sean sighed, massaged the side of his head, and struggled to sit up.

"You know I think these girls... Where the fuck are we?" Outside should have been the busy central London road that would take them all the way to their destination, not the dreary rows of houses of some north of the river estate. The shabby dwellings slouched against each other in their poverty; one in every five windows was boarded up. They passed under an old bridge, the graffiti on the walls like the decoration of a ghost train. When they came out the other side, tower blocks obscured any horizon, and the rows of the estate continued as if uninterrupted. It was, Sean thought, just like where they had come from.

"I don't know!" Tom said. "I missed the turning and then... I tried to... I thought there would be another... but when I tried it wasn't *right*, I stopped to ask someone and he said... but what he said didn't make *sense!* And I'm lost and..."

"Shit!" Sean said, "Shit, shit! If we're late... this guy isn't going to hang around forever waiting for us you know!"

"Oh who cares about the fence!" Tom cried. "What about the fat guy?" As he said this he wasn't concentrating, and there was the chastisement of a car horn, furious about something. In the rain, Sean couldn't even see the other car, or what it was they had done wrong.

"Would you shut up about him! The fat guy is just a figment of your retarded imagination!"

But the damage had been done – Sean couldn't stop himself thinking of the fat man, hearing his strange foreign voice, remembering the words he had spoken... – some of the words, at least.

The inside of the 'temple' had freaked Sean out, for the relics and religious ornaments had coexisted with other relics, relics of the normal and quotidian life that had apparently been lived here once. He had expected one back room to contain all the creepy stuff, not for it to be scattered haphazardly like catalogue knick-knacks on the tops of the TV and mantelpiece; not for the hideous murals to be draped from walls decorated with Eighties wallpaper; not for the ancient books to be stood up in the kitchen like they contained recipes. It was like seeing two things at once, one reality superimposed atop a second one, and his eyes seemed to itch as they attempted to decipher the puzzle. Sean and Tom had come with torches and this made things worse, for details of the temple kept emerging from the gloom as they turned their beams towards them: candlesticks, miniature statues, fluttering murals on the walls depicting impossible creatures: some showing combinations of existing animals such as rats and snakes, leeches and lizards. But others were beyond description, creatures formed from the usual stuff of tentacles, scales and hair, but in distorted and impractical forms it seemed impossible anyone could ever have conceived of. The worst thing about these idols had been the suggestion of sentience, somehow the very way they had been carved or painted implied a deranged and patient intelligence. Sean had tried hard not to look; tried harder to stop Tom jerking around and shining his torch at them every twenty seconds, convinced that they'd moved. Was the boy a liability? he'd thought. Had it been a mistake to bring him? They had both been sweating as they had hastily filled their bags with anything that looked valuable – but how were you supposed to tell, Sean thought, when it all looked like stuff from a poor B-movie? He found himself shoving it all in, trying hard not to look at the carvings and pictures, trying hard not to read the writing as the old and blasphemous books fell open in his hand... He would have felt more at ease robbing a *real* church for the imagery there would have been less disturbing...

When he had filled the first bag Sean ran out to the car, which was parked round the back of some garages. He'd seen Tom hadn't wanted to be left alone, but his friend was being slow filling up his bag, and Sean hadn't wanted to linger. Out in the cool night air Sean breathed a heavy sigh – from outside it was just a cramped ex-Council house like all the rest of them on the estate, and it seemed impossible to think of all the stuff he had seen inside. It seemed too small. He put his bag in the boot of the white family car, then got in and switched on the engine. But after another five minutes Tom still hadn't returned. Sean cursed – what was taking so long? They should have been in and out! He was angry, but there was an underlying feeling of panic that he didn't act on: if he had done he would have driven out of there alone.

Then Tom had rushed out of the temple (or house, or whatever the fuck it was) yelling and waving his arms. He had run to the car and got in the back, and shouted at Sean to go, while craning his neck to look behind him. He had been making enough noise to wake the entire street.

"Shut up!" Sean had whispered.

"Go Sean! Please!"

"What the hell's wrong?"

But all Tom seemed able to reply was:

"Fat man! I saw... the fat man!"

"What fat man? What the hell are you talking about?"

"The fat man! From Arkansas!"

At that moment Sean had made the decision never to do anything like this with Tom again – he understood why being in a place like that, where the trappings of everyday life didn't seem to sit sensibly next to the carved monstrosities and inverted religious symbols, where you weren't able to decide which aspect of your vision was false... Sean understood why a place like *that* could screw up your imagination. His own imagination had been screwed up, imagining the idols moving and the books falling open of their own volition... But Tom was seemingly unable to distinguish between what went on in his head and what was *real*; and where had this thing about a fat man come from? And he was obviously so upset he'd forgotten the *reason* they'd been there in the first place.

"Where's the bag, Tom?" Sean said.

"I must have... when the fat... when... the fat man!"

"Where the fuck's the *bag?*"

Tom flinched at Sean's anger.

"I dropped it! When the fat man came!"

Sean looked away, furious, trying to stop the shaking, trying to make the decision that he knew was the correct one: that it wasn't worth the risk of going back. If the stuff from the temple was worth anything then they already had enough to sell; and if it was all fake then it didn't matter how much they had. But he thought of the things he'd seen Tom put in his bag, glittering in his memory as if candle-lit, as if this were a real temple, with its treasures priceless...

"I'm going back for it."

"Sean, don't..." Tom whined, like a kid, still on the verge of tears. "What about... don't leave me! The fat man!"

Sean got out of the car, almost slamming the door with his anger until he remembered the situation. He ran back into the house (through the back door they'd forced earlier) and into its disjointed vision, the focus of his sight flicking between the flock wallpaper and the twisting shapes within its pattern. He stooped to pick up the holdall Tom had dropped in the front room, and even though it was dark he sensed a darker shadow falling over him. He cried out; he looked up.

"Hello," the fat man said, in an American accent.

He had been immense, every part of him bloated with what seemed a *deliberate* fatness, and not like someone who'd simply let himself go. Even his round glasses (in which Sean could see his stooped reflection) had seemed too big, like car headlights. His skin had been very red and shiny, very smooth as if it had been stretched tight and become sore. The fat man had no hair; his head had curved and gleamed. But it wasn't the physical details that had so scared Sean, but the same sense of itchy double-vision, the sense that what he was seeing was not the whole reality, but merely a gloss, a hasty camouflage.

Sean had wanted to run, but he hadn't been able to move a muscle. He had just remained bent over the loot, staring at the fat man and listening to his words: the fat man had spoken lightly, as though Sean was a stranger and this was just idle chatter at a bus stop. But his mouth had grinned with hidden meanings, and the words had nonetheless filled Sean with dread.

"I come from Arkansas, as you call it now. It was wild and vast and barren and empty then, you can't imagine. So empty, so different from now, when everywhere is filled with maggots like you, insignificant nothings. It would be tolerable if you knew your place, but when you trespass... do you know what happens to those who trespass?"

And after that Sean could remember nothing... except the vague idea that the most terrible thing that happened to those who trespassed against the fat man wasn't just that they died... or even how they died... but what happened to them *after* they died.

He told Tom none of this. After all, it had all been nonsense, there had been *no* fat man, how could there have been? If he had been anything other than a hallucination then Sean would never have been allowed out of the temple with the second bag. The fat man would simply have overpowered him or called the police. And since that hadn't happened surely that proved there had been no one there? And even if there had been, it could only have been a man, not anything else his imagination had read into the experience. It could only have been a man, and what could the fat bastard do to them now? As if in answer his mind flinched from the image of metal and glass slicing through him as the car hit the ground and crumpled...

He came back to the present; or rather, let what he could see take precedence over what he could picture. The back of the car felt claustrophobic, as did the maze of streets outside, the houses of the estate seemingly too close and leaning in. Tom was no longer pretending to hide his anxiety as he drove – his breathing was fast and shallow, his hands were clamped to the wheel as if it were trying to turn without him willing it.

"We're lost," he yelled. "I don't know where I am and everything looks the same! We've got to get out of here Sean, we've got to escape! But I don't know which way, there aren't any signs, it's all the same..."

"Concentrate on the road!" Sean yelled back; he pulled out the final cigarette from his packet.

"Would you stop fuckin' smoking!" Tom shouted, looking over his shoulder at Sean and almost swerving into the oncoming lane. With a cry Sean flung the fag down on the floor and stamped on it violently.

"There, that helps does it?" he said loudly. "Fucking pull over, let me drive." He wanted to be behind the wheel, to be in control.

There was a pause, during which Tom's panic subsided – he kept on driving but the only sound was the ragged way in which they were both breathing. Outside, the same shops went past as before, the same houses – or so it seemed.

"Sean?" Tom said finally, sniffing as he spoke.

"Yeah?"

"You *did* have those dreams didn't you."

"Sort of... yeah, sort of," Sean said.

"And you *did* see... see..."

"The fat man. Yes, I did."

"Oh God!" Tom shouted, his calm fading again.

"It doesn't mean anything!" Sean added quickly, not knowing who he was trying to convince most. "It was just a... a... a group hallucination!" he said, clutching at a phrase he'd read in the papers, about people who had seemed to see two things at once. "The fat guy – he wasn't real. How can he have been?"

"He wasn't real," Tom said quickly, and Sean realised with an appalled feeling that Tom was crying, and not bothering to hide it from him. "What we saw was just... I don't know, but it wasn't *him!* Not the *real* him! But he's still gonna get us and make us drive up that flyover and hit those kids and crash us and then..."

"Shut up! Shut up about that!"

"But it's going to happen! Oh fuck Sean, he'll get us and it's *all* going to happen!"

"Then don't stop!" Sean said. "Don't stop for anything – drive in one direction and let's get out of here!"

"It won't make any difference," Tom said quietly, but he sped up anyway. From the backseat Sean couldn't really gauge how fast they were actually going – he felt sick with a motion-sickness not helped by the way the houses seemed to slant as if the air through which he was viewing them was warped. He remember how as kids they'd once walked their bikes up the estate's steepest hill, called the Drop, how at the top they'd got on their bikes, turned round, and pedalled as hard as they could... He remembered the feeling half-way down that he couldn't stop now if even if he wanted to, that he'd committed himself to this crazy peer-pressure of speed and that to brake or even to steer now would throw him from the bike. And so he'd hung on half-terrified as the bike had plunged and rattled down the Drop. Now he felt like that, as the white car raced through the built up area, Tom taking corners in a way that felt barely under control. They went through a red light, and Sean instinctively flinched and closed his eyes as he felt the bray of angry traffic swerving to avoid hitting them side-on. But he didn't shout at Tom to slow down, for the idea seemed inconceivable and just as unsafe – they had to find a way out, keep moving, keep moving... Tom shouted something as he fought with the wheel, and the car mounted the pavement for a few seconds. Sean wasn't wearing his seat-belt, and he was flung to one side of the car, along with Rochelle and all the other models aping arousal. His head slammed against the door handle and he tasted sudden blood in his mouth as he bit his tongue. His heart hurt from the sheer speed it was beating at, as if willing the car faster and faster... Details of his dreams clouded his head: the riches he had taken, the inward shattering of the windscreen... He wasn't sure for a few seconds which was real and which wasn't. He tried to get up, but fell back as the car took another corner without braking. The roar of the motor and the sound of horns outside all seemed very loud, but he could still hear Tom chanting "Oh God, oh God..." under his breath. Bit late to start praying, Sean thought as they hit a straight section of road and Tom pressed down even harder on the accelerator. How fast were they actually going? It still didn't seem fast enough, even though outside was just a blur. Sean realised he was whimpering too. He struggled upright, half expecting to see a flyover in front of them and the smiling fat man in the passenger seat.

Instead he saw a long bus pull out blindly in front of them, blocking the road. Tom cried out, stamped on the pedal. The scream of the brakes drowned out Sean's own. He was thrown off the back seat again, twisting his hand painfully as he tried to break his fall. The car skidded for what seemed a long time; high pitched noises echoed around Sean's head. Then the car stopped and stalled.

And then all that happened was the bus driver and his passengers glared at them in fright, and what sounded like a thousand belated car horns were pressed at once. Then the bus drove slowly off, the traffic started to flow around them again. There were no pedestrians, the streets seemed deserted. Sean looked wildly round, just to make sure, but there was no one, no one at all. There was no fat American. The thought struck him all at once as ludicrous – there would be no American tourists in this rundown and aggressive estate of outer London. Sean flung back his head and laughed with relief. He heard Tom do the same. The fear that had made them want to go faster and faster fled at the laughter. He leant back against the car seat and let out a long drawn out breath which was like the madness escaping. He closed his eyes.

There was a tap at the window.

Sean's eyes flew open, but even closed they had already sensed the shadow which had fallen over him. A large, hunched form peered in through the passenger window. Sean impotently watched Tom lean over and unwind it. He could tell Tom desperately didn't want to, could tell by the expression of fright on his face, but reality had doubled and neither Tom's will nor his own had any interaction with it anymore – his limbs lay still as he commanded them to move. A stream of terrified thoughts flowed through his mind, but he did nothing. The window wound relentlessly down, revealing a huge face, fat hanging off, giant spectacles gleaming. Tom thought he saw the truth of that face for the first time, and when it spoke, it spoke in an American accent.

"Any chance of a lift?" the fat man said, and despite the raised last syllable, it wasn't a question.

JAMES EVERINGTON

HAUNTED

Eleanor could almost scream with frustration as she led the investigators round her house. They obviously didn't believe in the stories of the ghost, despite the history of violence and... murder.

Eleanor shuddered, and said to them that *here* was where it happened. But they didn't listen to a word she said! *Here!* she said and they barely even glanced in her direction.

Eleanor *did* scream as they turned to go. She screamed and the last of the investigators turned back with a frown... But then he shrugged, and shut the door, leaving Eleanor alone in the haunted house.

JAMES EVERINGTON

NEW BOY

He told himself that he wouldn't look up, wouldn't continue to look for something that wasn't there. But of course as he approached the grey office block his gaze lifted to the very top. It was an ugly, twelve-story building; but blank, with no discernible features to explain *why* it seemed so ugly. It just was. It imposed on the surrounding area by sheer height, not by being memorable – the sight of it on the local front page two weeks ago had been incongruous and had made him do a double-take.

He studied the straight line of the roof of the building, a razor cut against the blurred sky. It wavered in his vision as he stared. A car horn sounded, and he realised he was standing in the middle of the road, with his head craned upwards, eyes watering against the blur. Shaken, he ran up to the building and let himself in with a company swipe-card. Distantly, he heard sirens.

He walked through the lobby, plunged into the lift, and pressed the button for the top floor. The lift juddered upwards. He was a young man, but the photo on the swipe-card that was clipped to his belt was younger. Below his face was printed his name and rank: *Manager*. He was returning to work after a fortnight's absence, a 'paid suspension'. The lift continued to shake as it pulled upwards. Because of the mirrored walls, it seemed to the manager that the lift was packed full, but in fact he was sharing it with just one other person – both late. The manager's staff should already be at their desks. He pictured how they would turn to look at him as he entered, their eyes clear and harsh with altitude, looking down at him – he pictured this, but he had no idea of the picture's accuracy, for in truth he barely knew his staff. The youth in the lift with him could have been one of them and the manager wouldn't have known; but the boy scurried out at floor seven. The manager had to endure the climb to the top alone and with eyes closed, feeling like someone was breathing down his neck.

The floor on which he worked was open plan, except for two rooms sealed off at two of the corners – one his office, the other a storeroom. The rest of the floor was crammed with banks and banks of desks. There was a table to his left by the coffee machine and water cooler, and beyond that the fire-escape... After the gloom of the lift the twelfth floor seemed unnaturally bright, for there were windows letting in clear light on three sides, even though the day outside was rather drab. He shut his eyes. He heard innocuous work talk all around him, and he held his breath and tried to break the cipher – for surely they would really be talking about *him*. Opening his eyes, he found he had carried on walking, and he was now right up to one of the windows. The glass went almost all the way to the floor, so leaning forwards he could see the ground almost directly beneath him. The windows vibrated with the wind; he could see his reflection in the panes of glass sway with their movements, like he had suddenly been moved forward an inch; then back again.

He had two subordinates as direct reports, two sub-managers, and they were both huddled together in conversation and hadn't seen his return. The rest of his staff were temps hired from employment agencies – quick to get in, and quick to get rid of, if need be. As he looked around the twelfth floor he didn't recognise half of the faces – but he wouldn't have recognised them all two weeks ago either. It didn't mean they were new, it didn't stop him examining their faces a second, a third time... But that was just morbid, and he forced himself to stop. He called together his sub-managers into one of the corner rooms (*his* office) to let them know he was back, to see how they had coped in his absence. They looked at each other before they answered his questions. The manager felt they had coped rather *too* well.

"Have you got any new staff in?" he said. "Any... replacements?" He hated them for making him say it out loud.

The two glanced at each other.

"We've got someone starting today," one said. "A new boy".

"Good, good," the manager said. He knew that there was no one standing behind him, but he was resisting the urge to turn around because he knew there *was*, too. "I assume you can show this new kid what's what today? I imagine I have a lot of e-mails and reports to catch up on and..."

They chorused an affirmative and left. The door to his office rattled as it shut. Alone, the manager couldn't stop himself, and turned to look behind him. But all that was there was the window, the blank sky. He drew the blinds, anyway.

He didn't leave *early*, but it was frowned upon for managers to be seen leaving five minutes after their temps. But he'd had enough. He felt pursued even as he got into the empty lift. His reflections in the mirrored walls lined up behind him. Aided by gravity the lift seemed to plummet downwards, and he closed his eyes. Was it his imagination, or was it swaying slightly from side to side as well? His heart thumped when the lift stopped too early, for it seemed that it was between floors and that he would be trapped. But opening his eyes he saw it had just stopped at floor six to let someone else in.

He saw that it was *his* manager. She looked at him like she didn't know him. She stood on the other side of the lift, allowing space between them, allowing the other presence that only he could sense to insinuate itself between them – of course he knew there was no one else there *really*. The manager's manager got out at floor three. She wasn't leaving 'early' then. He didn't know whether her brief, chilly glance had been because he *was,* or because of what had happened two weeks ago. He left the tall building looking harried; and looking back.

The next day he made an effort to arrive early, although no one saw. He entered the office block, again after having lost the battle not to look up to its very top. He examined the faces of everyone in the queue for the lift – he knew what he was looking for was illogical; he didn't know what he would *say* if he found it. The lift doors opened and the crowd pressed in, mercifully hiding the double either side of him in the mirrored walls. On reaching the top floor the manager went straight to his office. Before, he had hardly ever used it, feeling that its small size didn't properly reflect his status. He had preferred to sit at one of the banks of desks, where everyone could see him. The office had really only been used for storing paperwork, and for firing people.

Unlike the open plan layout of the rest of the floor, his office only had windows on two sides not three; he had shut the blinds but the slats were old and uneven, and they still let in blades of light. He knew that the sky outside was a soothing grey colour, having taken on the character and hue of the satellite town beneath it. But still, as the blinds moved slowly with the movements of the thin windows he couldn't help but think that what was outside trying to get in was a cool, clear sky, a smokeless blue with a hint of breeze, and with alarm bells ringing somewhere far below or above him...

He realised that an alarm *was* ringing – it took him a few seconds to remember that this was the day that the fire-bell was tested, that this was a routine which he knew. Still, in those few seconds before he realised, his heart quickened until it seemed to beat with the pulses of the shrill alarm, and the manager wondered if it was happening again; and if that meant a reprieve or merely a repetition.

The bell stopped; his heart seemed to stop too. The swift silence didn't seem comforting, he was sure the echoes were still vibrating but too softly for him to hear. There was a surge and a clatter of high flying debris outside, sounding so close that he flinched... He stepped outside his office for some space, for some normality, but his vision felt blurred and his eyes quivered slightly – the blurring seemed to be a physical presence above and around him. The faces of his staff seemed to lurch from one expression to another as they looked up at him. He didn't recognise half the faces, and that was merciful; he didn't want to recognise *any*... – but then the room seemed to click back into focus and solidify. His eyes went fixed in their sockets.

The manager was watching one of the sub-managers, who was leant over a temp's desk, guiding him. The temp looked bored at what he was being shown, looked contemptuous at what he was expected to learn. He looked young and out of place in an office – a familiar look among the staff that the company hired (and fired). The manager felt a vertigo as a thousand things seemed to fall into focus... the temp's face refused to change. The manager beckoned his sub-manager over frantically.

"Who's *that?*" he said.

"The new boy. The replacement. Same kind of slacker as half the others but I'm sure he'll..."

"*Get rid of him!*" the manager said in a half-shrieked whisper, his eyes refusing to turn away from the bored, slack face that he had been looking for.

It had never been a problem for the manager to get rid of people before. He hadn't even needed to speak to the offending member of staff directly. It had been a simple case of waving to them cheerily as they'd left the office, and then calling the employment agency who had originally sent them. "I don't think he's working out..." "We were looking for someone with different skills..." And the agency would call the temp and explain; and they would send someone new in his place the next morning. All the employment agencies had so many ex-grads, drop-outs, and wannabes on their books that they never complained, for the money continued to flow as before, and they didn't want to lose custom. That was how it always had been.

"We can't just get rid of him," the sub-manager said, "for *nothing.*"

The manager shut his eyes, and felt the wind whip around the walls of his office. Here the walls seemed very thin, as thin as the rattling glass, and it was suddenly easy to remember that he was in fact standing hundreds of feet up in the air. On top of this, the manager's office was so small that with two other people in there it felt like he was being forced against the wall.

"Can't you *see* it?" he said, his own eyes still closed. Even so, he could sense the way the two of them glanced at each other before one of them spoke.

"I'm not saying there isn't a *similarity*," one said, "but Jay wasn't exactly *distinctive* looking anyway, so..."

Was it a conspiracy, the manager thought, or was it that the world had changed and only he could see it? For his subordinates did not seem to be able to see that the 'new boy' looked exactly like Jay had! (And Jay was the reason the manager had been off for two weeks.) It wasn't a 'similarity' or 'resemblance'; it was an exact match.

"Yeah, I mean they both have... had, that grungy hair, that slacker look," the other was saying, "but Jay was taller, and paler..."

"I don't care," the manager said, opening his eyes. The problem didn't matter so much, only the solution. "I don't care. Get rid of him. Call the agency. Or I'll do it myself."

"But we can't for *no reason*, he's still in training..." one said; "He's as good as any of the others, the agency will want to know *why*..." the other said. It was like he had come back to the wrong company, like this wasn't *his* office at all. He reached behind him to put a steadying hand against the wall, and almost shrieked as his hand seemed to pass *through* the wall and he felt himself falling... But all that had happened was that he had put his hand on the blind, whose slats had shifted and his palm had fallen against the vibrating window.

"Don't just ignore what I say," he said. "I'm in charge here, I set the agenda."

The two sub-managers took a step backwards, and he felt like he had reasserted something. Not just his higher rank, but something more – his view of the world perhaps, of the way things were, and should be. But then he saw them look at each other again, that little, confidence boosting, insubordinate *look* that they had developed in his absence. They never let him forget that in fact he had been at the company less time than they had.

"It was found that it wasn't my fault," he said suddenly. "That's what the inquiry found. That I was without blame."

There was no knock – the door to his office just opened and someone else pressed into its narrow confines. For a second, in the new light, he was sure it was Jay, or the 'new boy', come for him...

"Should you *all* be in here?" *his* manager said. "None of you outside looking after them?" She was looking at him coldly, her personality as smoothed-down and professional as her suit.

"We were discussing *them*," he said quickly. "Firing one of them. We could hardly discuss that out there." He noticed the two sub-managers glance at each other again.

"What's to discuss?" his manager said. "I won't ask who, I won't know them, but what have they done?"

"Nothing" – one of them, chipping in before he could speak. His manager looked away from him, turned her cool regard to them. He had a sense of things *slipping*, the feeling that if he closed his eyes and then opened them again things would be subtly, horribly different; the world would be tilted at a slightly different angle...

That feeling had started two weeks ago.

There had been a fire alarm – a shrill routine. His staff trudged dutifully down the fire escapes and then stood in clusters, smoking. He wore a fluorescent jacket and carried a clipboard with all their names on. He called the names out, and sometimes was surprised at the face that answered, for he had thought that face belonged to someone else. The manager ticked them off as he went down the list. At the end, one name was still unaccounted for.

He repeated the name once, twice, three times – he lost count. As he repeated it the syllables seemed to become more and more meaningless: "Jay Neuworth? *Jay* Neuworth? Jay New Worth?" Everyone just ignored him.

He was sure that Jay, or someone, was playing a trick in him, and he resolved to make sure that the boy's agency received a call to say that his services were no longer needed... But he was equally sure that there was no joke, and as he repeated the missing boy's name he felt his anxiety grow. He shook his head, like hitting a television set to restore the picture, and looked up at the building. The dull office block was reassuringly stable, with no smoke billowing out of its windows into the clear blue sky. Fireman had arrived but they were standing around with the security guards, discussing what had happened: had workmen accidentally cut the wrong wire, had one of the temps accidentally smashed the glass on one of the alarms? The manager's staff had taken the opportunity to smoke or gossip; his manager had formed her own clique away from him... No one was actually doing anything. "Jay Neuworth?" he said, his words a whisper. It was like his emotions were a few seconds further forward than events, for his stomach was churning and his eyes wavering.

Then someone had pointed upward, and screamed.

He came back into the present – it was as quick as a flick of the remote control; as disorientating as coming into a film halfway through. He knew that one of the sub-managers had just said "nothing" and flashed his colleague that quick glimpse of insubordination, but it seemed to have happened days ago. He tried to *focus*. There was, he realised, no way he could tell his manager that the new boy was Jay Neuworth's *double*, or as near as damn it – no way to tell her his guilt-tripped fantasies about what this doppelganger had come for. No way to tell her, but maybe a way to make her *see*. She wouldn't have known Jay from the toilet cleaners, but she would have seen his face in the newspaper. He glared at Tweedle-Dum and Dee – they might be pretending that they couldn't see it, but surely *his* manager wasn't part of their lowborn conspiracy?

"Come with me," he said. "*Look*". He had to squeeze past her to get to his office door – he felt her body stiffen, and press back against the thin partition wall, which wobbled. Their arms brushed each other and he got a hint of her scent. It was always a relief to be out of his cramped office, although the twelfth-floor light confused his eyes after his dark cubby hole – almost a relief, until he saw *him*, the new boy. But still, he tried to obey his own imperative, he tried to *look*:

The boy was probably in his mid-twenties, with a slack face, bored eyes. His hair was lank, even his skin seemed lank, seeming to slouch down from his skull with not much in the way of defining muscle in between. He had taken full advantage of the company's casual dress policy for the temps, and wore a t-shirt that was too big for him and slumped from his frame, so that the legend *Touch Me I'm Sick!* which presumably should have emblazoned his chest, was creased into his gut. Everything about the kid seemed pulled downwards, except his eyes which looked upwards from his bowed head, with a bored and solipsistic intelligence... He...

And he looked exactly like Jay Neuworth! The feeling of vertigo and sudden slippage overtook him again. *Exactly like...* it was all his brain could hold onto, in this new rendering of things.

One look at his manager was enough to tell him that she couldn't see it.

He thought – maybe those two can't see it either. Maybe it wasn't a conspiracy, but a sign. *Only* he could see it.

His manager was looking at him, expecting something. His mind, which already felt like it was struggling with two versions of reality, couldn't lie and create a third. If only he could find some plausible reason to get rid of the boy! But all he said was,

"I just... I don't like the look of him, that's all. He looks lazy and likely to turn up late, and..." It was true as far as it went. *Jay* had always turned up late.

"You can't get rid of someone just because you don't like the look of them," his manager said. "This department has targets to reach. I know you've only just come back after... but *still*." Her professional, unflappable countenance cracked, flapped for a second, like a vision of her twin self. "But *still*," she repeated.

The manager looked away from her, back at the new boy. "What's his name?" he heard his manager ask his subordinates behind him, and whichever one responded, the answer they gave jarred wrong in his head.

~

He forced himself not to hide all week in his office, but to sit at a desk in among everyone else. He flinched every time the new boy passed near, but fortunately he didn't have to have anything directly to do with him. The one time he did sit in his office he didn't get any work done, he just kept irritably drawing the blinds, then opening them minutes later, as if there was something outside that was a temptation. He needed to get some work done, he needed to get back into the swing of things to counter whatever insurrection and arse-licking his sub-managers were planning. He needed to catch up; he needed to *work*...

He sat at his desk and watched the 'new boy'.

It wasn't just that he looked like Jay Neuworth – he *moved* like him too. He moved in a way that was seemingly indolent, but also suggested speed and aggressiveness were there if needed, like a slow throw-back, a reptile. The boy didn't blink enough, despite the fact that light was battering against the windowed walls. There was a faint noise of alarm from the manager's computer as he made these observations, a reminder for a management meeting three floors down.

He watched how the other temps interacted with the 'new boy' too, after all it was conceivable that some of them had been Jay's friends. Surely they would notice? He didn't know which ones to watch, didn't understand the friendships and rivalries among his team, but none of them appeared to be acting in anything other than a natural way around the new boy.

During the course of his observations he noticed some of his staff committing acts that were against company rules – one looking at a website while she should have been working, one who blatantly had twice as many fag breaks as anyone else, one who just sat and stared out the window without working for minutes at a time... No one could complain if he sacked *them* (the new boy didn't put a foot wrong). He did the sackings face to face, in his small office, rather than just calling the employment agencies, and he made the sub-managers attend too. It was strangely calming, it reassured him that he could actually influence reality, rather than just watch its patterns and jumps in front of him.

Still, every time he went into his office to fire someone he noticed how much it was *moving*, how much the building moved. He had never realised tall buildings could move before, with the wind, with the tremors. He noticed the movement out in the open plan part of the office too, but out there it was like being on a ferry in a rough sea; in his office it was like being in a dingy. Even the vibrations from his ringing phone seemed to set the movement off – he switched it to silent.

One boy actually *cried* when they sacked him. The manager felt a moment's pride as he watched the idiot scuttle away to collect his things and say his goodbyes. All the other temps were watching him out of the corners of their eyes. Including *him*, with the coldly amused eyes of someone who had just seen yet another arrow fall short of its target.

"I'm going for a piss," he said, not even aware that he had spoken aloud. The two sub-managers glanced at each other. The manager stood still for a few seconds longer, then walked off.

It took a long time for him to relax and to be able to piss. He was in one of the cubicles, and there was a draft around his ankles, because the cubicle wall didn't reach to the floor. The sliding bolt to lock the cubicle had a screw loose and was almost hanging off – it all seemed very fragile. He sighed and felt the movement of the air shuddering out of his body. He closed his eyes, listened to the welcome silence.

The door to the toilet opened and he heard shuffling footsteps on the other side of the cubicle wall. The manager blinked and his trickle of coffee-clear pee dried up. He heard a cough, them someone spitting phlegm into a urinal. He heard unzipping then a stream of piss – something marking its territory, he thought.

He told himself that of course there was no way of knowing who it was; and even if he did know what did it matter? Still, he hugged his knees up to his chest, so that his feet wouldn't be visible in the gap beneath the cubicle wall.

The sound outside stopped and he heard someone zipping themselves up. Then they moved to the sinks, which were even closer to his cubicle – he almost flinched in physical aversion to the person just a few meters away. He heard the sound of someone washing their hands, then the sound of the automatic hand drier – a roaring, wind-like noise that hid any sounds of the person moving outside. His heart faltered then sped up. The sound of the drier was on for a long time, then stopped. There was no noise from the other side of the cubicle. The person must have left. Still, the manager wasn't sure that he wanted to unlock the door quite yet. For some reason he had the fear that he would throw open the door and see a slightly different world, or a different face in the mirror. But gradually he relaxed. He put his aching legs back on the ground.

Suddenly the door to the toilet cubicle shook, rattling on its hinges. Someone was shaking it from outside, trying to get in! His mind convulsed and stammered the three syllables of Jay Neuworth's name. He shrank back on the toilet and gave a cry of fear. The door rattled again, and the screw holding the bolt in place became even looser. Not that it mattered, for there was splintering wood around the other screws too: one way or the other it was getting in...

The rattling stopped as suddenly as it had started. He remained still with his trousers around his ankles, but he didn't hear anyone walking away.

~

The e-mail was dated four days previous, and from his manager. The title of it was *Re Our Previous Talk* but he hadn't yet opened it to read the contents. Before he finally did so he looked around, to make sure no one was behind him, watching. For he felt that there was, and worse than watching, they were moving forward with palms raised...

The first thing he noticed about the mail was that it had been sent out to his sub-managers too. The sight of their names irritated him, and he looked around again. Then he read the mail, and he couldn't believe it. The phrases swam before his tired eyes:

...obviously out of touch with your staff, old and new, since your absence... after what has happened, team spirit needs to be rebuilt and that is your... a team nigh out... out of the budget... For all three of the senior members of the team, attendance is of course required. The date for the proposed night out was four days after the mail had been sent; the night was tonight.

The manager stood up, and felt his vision waver. He laid a hand against the office wall to steady himself, and felt it vibrate under his trembling palm. Outside, the wind howled; a siren sound raced far below him...

Then someone had pointed upwards, and screamed.

He turned to look. His eyes travelled up the office block, looking for flames or billowing smoke, looking for a red sky lit behind, heralding disaster. But its walls and windows were as grey and meaningless as ever, and his eyes strained over its dull surface looking for something that might have caused someone to cry out like that. The screaming continued behind him, but he saw just the building stark and sharp-edged against the clear blue. But then his gaze swung right to the *very* top, above the twelfth-floor windows, to the roof, and he saw what he had been looking for.

And here it had started, for the building started swaying in his vision.

At the top of the building was a figure. And the manager took an involuntary step backwards, for it felt like *he* was on the roof and looking down... But instead, the figure was looking down, and it was familiar to him. He could see the slouched posture, the lank hair being whipped by the wind into an unruly and wavering mane. He didn't know exactly who it was, but he knew it was someone for whom he was responsible. The screams and shouts increased; the manager could sense movement and sounds of fear behind him.

How had Jay got up there? By one of the fire-escapes? Of course, the manager thought with an odd calmness, he had opened one of the fire-doors to get up there, and that was what had set off the alarms. What was he *doing* up there? Logically, he could be preparing to unfurl an anti-CO_2 banner or make some other kind of protest, and part of him was yet again planning to call the temp agency... But equally, the part of him that was absorbing all the fear and panic of those behind him knew this was no protest. And this double-vision of the brain persisted even as the figure took its first step towards the edge of the building.

It took three steps – they didn't appear to be dramatic or decisive, just shuffles, like someone dawdling to a job that they didn't like, and then the figure was falling. Just three everyday steps, and the figure had looked *behind* him whilst taking the last one... As easy as walking into the road looking in the wrong direction. The figure had been up on the roof for only a few moments; not long enough for the firemen to be halfway there; not long enough for any negotiations or explanations. The boy's fall seemed drawn out and insidious, falling in the manager's vision slowly and even lazily. There seemed to be little momentum; the fall didn't seem *irredeemable* but something that could be reversed even at this late stage.

And then the boy hit the ground and then there was very little left to see. Time sped up again. The firemen rushed forward, both blocking his view of what now lay on the pavement, and turning to avoid seeing it themselves. *How dare he?* he thought idiotically. The manager stepped backwards, and almost tripped. His clipboard fell to the floor. Turning around, he found that it was his manager that he had backed into. She had been looking at him; they had *all* been looking at him, his sub-managers and the whole pack of the rest of them, swaying in his vision like landmarks glimpsed from sea. He had wanted to look away from everyone, but the clear and bright day that engulfed him when he did so had been somehow worse....

Attendance is of course required, he thought, with his hand against the office wall. So that was when it would happen, whatever 'it' was. He walked out his small office and looked at the 'new boy'; and Jay Neuworth looked back at him with the same blank look in his eyes that he must have had falling... The manager went back into his own office, and tried to work late.

Instead he looked out the window at the city below him which seemed to grow sharper in his vision as he watched – the light from the setting sun was clear and highlighted the differences between things, the jagged edges. It was like looking down from cliffs to the rocks below. I'm on the top-floor, he thought, Jay was on the roof. It's pretty much the same view.

It took an effort of will to draw the blind and turn away. He heard the temps and the rest of the staff leave, but he stayed hours after that, managing not to work. He left the building to go straight to the team night out, still wearing his creased and inappropriate day clothes, the company swipe-card the manager needed for access still clipped to his belt.

A team night out? His mind felt incredulous at the suggestion. It couldn't be that he was going to spend *voluntary time* with his staff. He barely knew them after all; and more than that, the new boy might be there, that skin-crawling doppelganger...; he should just go home, but his mind felt incredulous at that suggestion too: *your attendance is of course required etc.* ...He went out into the evening light still not knowing exactly what was awaiting him, which punishment he would choose. The streets seemed crazed, the traffic murderous. People dashed to cross the road at the scantest opportunity, while he scuttled back and forth across the curb not daring to cross. It was a new fear for him, of stepping out into the road; the green man took an age coming and people walked passed him and dodged traffic, except for the old who muttered beside him. When he crossed he felt as slow as them, and felt too like he only just made it across before the lights changed and the engines revved. It didn't help that while he had been waiting to cross it had felt like something was urging him, almost pushing him, forward. Just a few steps. The streets felt crazed; but he realised they had always been like this, too.

He noted his destination with blank surprise – so he had been heading here, after all. In front of him, across another treacherous road, was an ugly modern building, all fragile glass it seemed, containing gyms, multiplexes, bars. Even from this distance he could see the innards, the people inside. When he finally entered, he found that the bar that he wanted was on the third floor, and he had to get an escalator which was glass sided and at a steep incline. It felt like it was tipping backwards and he felt sick; his vision bobbed and doubled as if he were already drunk. When he reached the third floor and headed towards the bar the manager felt like the escalator was still carrying him forwards.

Sunlight – the bar had, of course, huge glass windows to share the view of cambered rooftops and climbing spires. He closed his eyes instantly, but red and green shapes like another reality danced behind his eyelids when he did. His ears detected a phantom rattling; he felt he could feel the wind blowing through the windows. Was it really only three stories up? Had he really come to this bar at all? In another universe, he thought, I went home and never came here.

In amid the doubling shapes of evening light that baffled his vision, people were beckoning him – he didn't know their names. Out of work the temps looked different, dressed funny and with uninhibited faces. His sub-managers were sitting in among them, with the same naked smiles, no doubt encouraging insurrection. But the manager didn't care for he saw that *the new boy wasn't there* and it didn't matter that his senses were telling him that there was someone behind him reaching out because there *wasn't* and...

There was a tap on his shoulder. He gave a little cry, turned around. He was so used to seeing Jay everywhere that when he saw him his mind waited for the face to dissolve into someone else, before realising that that wasn't going to happen.

"Drink?" said the new boy. "My shout?" His voice was exactly the same as Jay Neuworth's slurred voice, and full of threat. The manager took a step backwards, away, into the sunlight that was pouring through the windows. People were looking at him. Behind the new boy he saw *his* manager come into the bar, dressed as straight-laced as ever; she paused, searching for a second, then headed towards him.

"Drink?" the boy repeated stubbornly.

He wondered why, since he had spent the last few weeks looking for Jay Neuworth everywhere, he had never given a thought to the circumstances of his life, only the manner of his death.

"Bitter?" he managed, his voice a strangulated gasp. "Bitter?" The new boy gave a smile – "Yes," he said, "bitter" – and headed away towards the bar.

The manager felt trapped – he didn't want to sit down , for he felt if he did then the temps on the sofa would pen him in, keep him pressed down if he needed to rise urgently. Instead he remained standing, pretending to look around the bar; a nerve jumped in his eye. The bar was modishly characterless, glass-top tables lit up like mirages in the sun from the large windows; the bar itself set back in the murk. He could hear the new boy talking to the barmen there but couldn't make out the words. To the right of the bar, also in the dark light, were three doors: *Ladies*, *Gents* and...

"Nice to see you here," *his* manager said; she had somehow moved right behind him without him noticing. He felt like reality kept twitching and changing with no prior warning. As he traded polite clichés with his manager, he felt like he was in fact saying something else, to a different person.

"You've obviously had a few before you came here," his manager said, with a professional expression of humour and tolerance. But she sniffed as if she could smell the alcohol on him – when he hadn't even had a single drink yet! The thought reminded him that the boy – that *Jay* – would be returning from the bar soon.

"Excuse me," he interrupted. "I'm sorry." I have to get out of here, he thought. The new boy was handing money over at the bar... The manager turned and hurried towards the door marked *Gents*.

The window was open in the toilets (which were about three times the size of his office) and he could feel the cool air creeping in; hear the sounds of the city below him. He didn't know why he had come in here, it was nothing more than a temporary reprieve. A hot terror was rising in him; he stuck his head under the tap but the water was warm and didn't wash away the feeling. The mirror in front of him was cracked and doubled his reflection; made him think someone else had entered the gents behind him. He turned around, his eyes blind and full of water, and walked directly through the space where he'd thought he'd seen someone. In another universe, he thought, I never came here, and this isn't happening.

He exited the toilets cautiously. Looking around he couldn't see the boy anywhere: not at the bar, not sitting in among his colleagues. The temps were silhouetted against the window; *his* manager was standing to one side and looking at him. The feeling that he had to leave before he did something terrible increased. Where *was* the new boy? He looked to his left, at the signs on the other two doors: *Ladies* and *Fire Exit. Only to be Opened in Emergencies.*

Until he pushed the bar to open the door, he hadn't realised his exit would set off the building's alarms. The familiar sound caused him to pause – he was still on the verge of being able to claim it was an accident, to go back and sit down. But the pause was mental only, like the gap between jumping and landing, because he was already rushing down a rickety metal fire-escape. The ground looked a thing impossible to reach; the view was like he was falling. The alarm rang above his head, and he heard noises of protest, the beginnings of pursuit. As he fled down the fire-escape his steps were panicked, but cautious, like an old man's, shaking as the metal shook beneath him. Even when he set foot on solid ground it seemed to be shaking.

There was an angry shout above him – he looked up and saw a black figure looking down at him. He could see nothing more because of the white light above him. The manager lowered his gaze and quickly looked around his surroundings.

The alleyway was a dark, hot corridor, between what seemed to be two walls of light at either end. The way back to his house was to the right; so was the sun and the still blue sky. Turning left was darker. Above him he heard the fire-escape start to rattle again, whether with the wind or because someone was coming down after him he didn't know. He turned left, and ran.

There was a road at the end of the alley and he found his fear of traffic returning. There was nowhere to cross, and the traffic seemed a constant flow, a tidal movement of speeding metal (it didn't occur to him *why* he wanted to cross, why he didn't just turn left or right and flee along the pavement). But concurrent with his fear was the feeling of someone pushing him, urging him forwards into the road...

There was a screeching sound and he looked up and saw that a bus had stopped to let him cross. The driver's face seemed to alternate between generosity and hate as he made a get-on-with-it gesture. The manager stepped off the lip of the curb gingerly, like he was tight-rope walking across a drop. He was aware of the growling bus to his right, aware that if it was a trick and the bus suddenly moved forward he wouldn't have time to react. He knew the idea was ridiculous but he started to run anyway – into the other lane, which he had temporarily forgotten was there – cars screeched and honked and seemed to miss him by inches as he suddenly appeared from behind the bus. He was shaking when he got to the other side of the road – he felt like he was going to be sick.

He turned around; on the other side of the traffic he saw the boy, who was trying to cross, but kept having to pull back because the flow of cars refused to pause. When the boy saw the manager looking at him his expression turned urgent, almost eager. The manager watched the boy try to cross again, saw Jay Neuworth's face shout something at him, but the words were lost in the sound of the traffic. "I'll *fire* you!" the manager shouted, his voice shrill. "I'll call the agency and..."

The manger jerked away from the roadside awkwardly, feeling a stitch on one side dig into him. He ran up one side of the street. There was an opening into another alleyway, and he ducked into it, feeling slightly comforted by its cramped, dark confines. But he had to keep running, because he felt that because he was no longer in the office, because of the strange parallel-world decisions he had made that evening, then no rules applied anymore, and the thing coming after him would have no restraints. There was a contrary urge in him to stop and *explain*; but he had no idea what he should say to Jay, and two weeks compulsive brooding had not given him an answer. He fled deeper into the alleyways.

He thought he would be safe after sunset, but it was dark when it got him.

He was walking up a quiet street in an unsavoury area, which ran parallel to the main road and was lined with adult bookstores, chippies, and pubs that most never dared drink in. He couldn't run anymore, he was too tired, instead he moved in a quick and painful shuffle. He wasn't sure if anything was still behind him – when he turned to see his eyes could only penetrate so far into the night. Everything was blurred and wouldn't come together. His hands had unconsciously unclipped his work ID card from his belt and were turning it over and over.

When he next looked up, someone was in front of him.

His first thought was one of relief, despite the edge of light on the knife that the figure held in its hand. This was just a person, not Jay Neuworth or anything like him. He studied the man's face – pale, with short cropped hair, a piddling little mustache. The man appeared to be shaking slightly in agitation – his knife blade wavered in and out of the light. The man was staring at him with eyes that looked doped, duped...

The familiar sensation hit him when he looked at the man's eyes – another world seemed to step out from behind the one he was seeing. The slack, bored look of malevolence was familiar, and so were the lazy steps that the figure took towards him.

"C'mon, are you *deaf*? Give your wallet!" The voice *was* Jay Neuworth's, despite the differences in pitch and timbre. "Now!" There was a gesture with the knife; light flashed.

The manager opened his mouth to protest – this didn't seem quite right. Why had there been an insinuating presence *behind* him these last few weeks, if Jay had just been planning to step out in front of him, crudely waving a knife? "No," he said, "no." Something wasn't correct.

That slack face tightened for a second, the gaze grew alert as if suspecting a trick. "What you on about man?" But then there was a relapse, the return of stoned malevolence. "Just gimme your wallet!"

"No," the manager repeated. "You *fell*. You can't just stab me..." The manager's voice was stronger, because he was convinced that this didn't fit with what *should* happen.

He heard a noise of impatience. "The fuck I can't." The world tilted, like he was back in a tall building moving with the high wind. Maybe he was. The world was at right-angles to where it should be in his vision – he was aware of distant pain. He kicked his legs trying to get away, as he saw Jay Neuworth bend over him, hands eager.

It wasn't like waking up and realising it was a dream. There was no simple transition from one state to another, instead there was a movement back and forth, a swaying from one view of the night to another as he staggered home, the path rising and falling like a fairground ride; neon lights and pub names doubled meanings in front of him, far away people crashed into him or propositioned him. His fingers were pressed tightly against the knife wound – which *might* just have been a pain in his side from drinking too much. Had his drink been spiked? He remembered the new boy Jay handing him a pint and grinning with uncharacteristic alertness as he had sipped it, and he had vowed to sack him at the first opportunity... But he *also* remembered fleeing the bar sober, having not had a drink, and the invisible pursuit through the alleys, and the *cold* feeling of the knife just below his ribs... He steered a course between these two sets of memories, based on a amalgamation between them, which maybe wasn't right. His head seemed to ache with effort.

No one was *following* him, there was no presence behind him anymore. No, he felt like the presence was somewhere in front of him now, and in his unfocussed, reeling way he plunged towards it. Looking up, there were a myriad of lights above him, rotating on an axis that he couldn't see, and the sight made him dizzy, and his steps faltered...

And then he was in his bed, and all he was thinking about was the horrible way that that boy, Jay Neuworth, had fallen from the top of the building...; then he rolled the wrong way and felt a convulsive pain in his side. He vomited over the side of the bed, and passed out or fell asleep again. When he awoke the world still lurched between clarity and hangover; between sick guilt and the pain from his wound.

He knew that he wasn't going into work and that he should call in sick, but he turned onto his good side and closed his eyes instead, desperate for a respite from the way the world slid from one state to another before his nauseous eyes.

It was two weeks afterwards when he returned. He told himself that he wouldn't look up, wouldn't continue to look for someone who wasn't there. He ducked his head and shielded his eyes as he approached the grey office block. His swipe-card no longer worked, but one of the security guards recognised him and let him in. But then he said "Know where you're going sonny?" so maybe he *wasn't* recognised. "Yes," he said, "twelfth floor," and he plunged into the lift.

The empty lift shook as it climbed upwards. He looked at its paper-thin metal walls and imagined them fading away, so that he could see the drop that he was slowing being raised above. He thought of the wind outside *his* office, the cool air, the rattling fragile windows.

He stepped out the lift onto the twelfth floor, his mind curiously blank. There was nothing sensed behind him, that was all gone now. He wondered just what Jay Neuworth had been *feeling*, what terrors and vertigo, but such thoughts were no good now. He lowered his head. He walked towards his office, ignoring the glances from unknown temps. The 'new boy' was no longer there; or at least, there was no one there with Jay's appearance anymore. The manager wasn't surprised. The idea of some doppelganger, some revenant, had fallen away like a mirage in a world that had returned to being clear and steady and...

He opened the door to his office, and saw one of the sub-managers sitting behind his desk. The light from the windows behind stung the manager's eyes — someone had removed the blinds, and rearranged the furniture.

"Christ," the sub-manager said, "you're supposed to be..." The manager stepped forward angrily, feeling confused by the way the familiar room looked completely different. The feeling of double-vision came back and he almost raised his fists; but he stopped as the door behind him opened. The hair on the back of his neck pinpricked and he felt the last two weeks drop away. He felt sick and tearful again. The boy's note had cited harassment and bullying at work; people who didn't even know his name threatening to fire him. But surely *he* had done nothing wrong, he had barely even spoken...

The manager took a step backwards, jerkily. *His* manager was behind him. "Ah," she said. "Didn't you get our letter? How did your swipe-card work, it should have been deactivated..." The company had a policy of making people easy to sack, from *his* manager's staff downwards.

He wanted this double-vision that felt like blindness to end; he wanted the guilt even though he had done nothing wrong to end. The door was still open behind him, and in another world he no doubt left through it... He felt a rush of cold air, felt the tall building sway and rattle. The windows shook with the wind. He felt gentle, almost inviting hands on his back. In front of him was a rectangular gleam of cold clear light – the windows had always seemed fragile, never more so. There was a very tiny increase in pressure. He took one step forward, a second, then lurched to a third. Almost a run... He felt his legs tense in preparation, and he lowered his head to expose his neck.

There was a feeling of cold air, and everything seemed to coalesce in one direction. Somewhere far above or below him, an alarm screeched. So *this* is what it felt like, he thought. So this is what I do deserve, after all.

THE TIME OF THEIR LIVES

Vince thought he was the only kid staying at the hotel, until he saw the girl at breakfast. Normally he wouldn't have made eye contact, for he was a naturally shy boy and she looked a year or two older than him. And she was a *girl*. But twenty-four hours of seeing nothing but grown up faces (and wrinkly ones, at that) made him reckless and he risked a smile, a little wave.

The girl smiled too, but nervously, and she didn't pause in the chewing of a strand of her long hair. She was sitting at a table in the corner of the hotel dining room, with a shrunken looking old lady who had one crooked hand laid possessively on the girl's knee. Vince noticed they both had a congealed and completely uneaten fried breakfast in front of them, before his own grandma pulled his hand and led him to a free table. From his seat Vince couldn't see the girl anymore. His grandfather was hovering, dithering behind him.

"Alfred sit down!" his grandma snapped tiredly. Vince's granddad did so. He looked around.

"Where are we?" he said. He glanced at Vince suspiciously, but didn't say anything else. Vince's grandma made a sound halfway between a tut and a sigh.

A waiter appeared, fresh faced and grinning, as if tending a room full of cantankerous old people was *just* how he liked to start his morning. Vince ordered the full English (because his parents weren't here to tell him no) as did his grandfather. They both wolfed it down when it came, although his granddad looked a little surprised at its arrival. His grandma stirred a spoon through her figs and cereal, stained her lips with tomato juice. She was ill in some unspecified way that Vince didn't understand, and he'd been told to make allowances for her.

After he'd finished, Vince started to fidget – the quiet, stealthy sound of all the old people eating around him made him feel unsettled; the occasional shout by a loud voice into a deaf ear made him jump. The hotel's dining room, with its blotchy wallpaper and shabby carpet looked old; it *smelt* old, as if the same old meals just kept getting reheated and served again, because none of the old-timers actually ate them...

The young waiter stood aside to let them pass as they left, but he didn't smile or even look at Vince (who was after all closest to the waiter's age) but only at his grandparents. He had a greasy face, Vince noticed, as if he'd applied some kind of ointment minutes before. He said something to his grandma about "the evening's entertainments" but Vince wasn't really listening (what entertainment would there be in a dump like this anyway?) because he was looking for the girl. But she was gone; her breakfast was still untouched, and as the waiter went to collect the plates his grandma laughed nervously at something he'd just said, and his grandfather loudly complained that he didn't understand who that man was.

Vince's mum and dad had seemed nervous when they had proposed that he go on holiday with his grandparents; Vince had been nervous too, for he'd heard them arguing about it the night before, when they'd thought he'd been asleep. Their angry voices had woken him, and he'd sneaked to the top of the stairs to listen.

He didn't know why all the shouting; he'd been on holiday with granddad and grandma before, so why shouldn't he again?

But his Mum (they were her parents; both his grandparents on his father's side had died before he'd been old enough to remember them) started crying. Vince couldn't tell what she was saying but his father's next words were uncertain and had lost their conviction.

"It's too much," he said, "for a boy of Vince's age... For Vince."

The next morning, while his Mum was packing his case, his Dad had made sure Vince had his mobile number and whispered to him: "Promise to call if anything happens to your granddad or grandma."

But nothing had happened, to them or anyone else as far as Vince could tell – by the end of their first full day they'd exhausted the possibilities of the quaint Cotswolds village – the tea rooms, the model village, the ducks on the river. Vince had permission to go off alone as long as it wasn't far, and he'd found an old arcade machine in the local chippy – its graphics not just worse than those of his games console at home, but worse than the one he'd had before that. Nevertheless he fed ten pence pieces into it, building up extra lives until his grandma came to drag him back to the hotel for dinner.

He didn't see the girl, or her grandmother, all day.

Back at the hotel he went to his room – at first the idea of his own hotel room had been exciting, but that had been another novelty that had lasted less than a day. For a start, he hadn't realised how much time he'd have to spend *in* the room, because his grandparents rested so often, and insisted he did the same. And it was an old person's room – a carpet with the pattern faded out, doilies on the dresser, a painting of a stag not quite straight on the wall. A fly lay stiff on its back on the window sill. And an old, ticking clock that kept Vince from thinking straight. A door connected his room to his grandparents' – they could unlock it from their side, but there was no key on his.

The second night, he'd just about got used to the ticking clock when the noise started – it took him a few seconds to identify it as music, for it was muffled and had a scratchy, trebly quality, like it was being played on old-fashioned equipment. And it was old-fashioned music too – Vince didn't know how old, but it made him think of black and white film of pre-war dances.

Despite its muffled nature the music was *loud*, coming from somewhere on the floor below. Vince looked at the gap underneath the connecting door to see if it had woken his grandparents, but there was no light on in their room. They were both somewhat deaf, he remembered, and slept with earplugs in.

A waltz, Vince thought, a jive, is that what they call this kind of music? Was it *meant* to be this loud and distorted? He knew he wouldn't be able to fall back to sleep while it was playing.

He got out of bed and walked across the room in the dark (he didn't want to risk his grandma seeing a light through the door and knowing he was up). He cautiously opened the room door – outside, the deserted hotel corridor seemed to pulse and shimmy with the music's beat. He was surprised it didn't seem to have woken anyone else.

Making sure he had his room key in his pyjama pocket, Vince quietly shut the door behind him, and cautiously went down the spiral stairs to the lobby. There was no one around, no one complaining at the reception. There weren't any lights on, and the air was grey as if full of dust; Vince's friend at school had told him dust was made up of dead people's atoms, but Vince wasn't sure if he believed him.

There was a pause in the music, and Vince thought he heard cheers and applause – even those sounds were scratchy, as if just old recordings. The music started again – was it the same tune, Vince wondered; it all sounded the same to him, old music, but wasn't it *exactly* the same tune?

The music was coming from the back of the hotel lobby, where there was an old carved wooden door, marred with an incongruous plastic *Staff Only* sign. Vince cautiously moved towards the door and put his ear to it. The music seemed to be simultaneously coming from behind the door and to be muffled by distance, as if the door opened not onto the hotel kitchen or office, but onto a vast, echoing, empty plain, where the same tune repeated itself until devoid of meaning... Vince didn't dare try the doorknob to see if it was locked or not.

Stepping away, he noticed two small faces carved into the old wood of the door – Vince had learnt about those faces at school, the theatrical masks of Comedy and Tragedy. These ones were heavily stylised – the weeping face of Tragedy was deeply lined and its open mouth showed one peg-tooth. Comedy was smooth-faced and its mouth was flung open in a manic grin. But Vince didn't like it so much – the grin seemed too wide, too strained, too full of boisterous and uncontainable desires. Someone who grinned like that might do *anything*. Comedy also seemed to be weeping, although with laughter, Vince supposed.

He felt hands on his shoulders and whirled around in the grey darkness...

The girl he'd seen at breakfast yelped and jumped back. He flinched at the noise, although surely no adult would be able to hear it over the music. They both stared at each other uncertainly for a few seconds. Then the girl beckoned him forward and cupped her hands round his ear to speak to him. She was just wearing a nightdress and her bare arm brushed his.

"This happens *nearly* every night," the girl said into his ear, her breath tickling. "Not last night, when you arrived, but every other night I've been here."

"What does your gran... grandma say about it?" Vince asked, speaking back into her ear. He could smell shampoo in her hair, and he briefly noted that it smelt nice, before wondered why he'd think such a thing.

"My granny says she doesn't hear it," the girl said. "She says I'm making it up! She sleeps in another room to me so I'm not sure if she *really* can't hear it."

"How... how long have you been here?" Vince asked.

"About a week. Two more days to go, ughhhh!" She paused, looked nervously at her bare feet then back at Vince. "I know you came yesterday because there's no other kids here, so I noticed you." She looked around the hotel lobby which still echoed with the music. "I better get back, I don't want to get into trouble. What's your name?"

"Vince," he said, "what's..?"

"Alice," the girl said, and turned and ran – although she looked older than Vince she still ran like a kid, an unsteady, clattering sprint up the wooden stairs. After a few seconds, Vince followed her, but she was already out of sight.

The next morning at breakfast Vince was going to ask his grandparents if they'd heard the music, but the thought of what Alice had said about her grandmother stopped him. It wasn't that he didn't trust his grandparents, rather that he had the odd thought that Alice wouldn't want him to speak about it, and the even odder thought that if Alice didn't want him to do something, then *he* didn't want to do it.

His grandma *looked* like she'd been kept awake all night by something, for she kept yawning and even ordered a coffee (a drink Vince had never seen her drink before) but she didn't mention the music. Nor did she seem in bad spirits despite her tiredness; she was smiling more than usual. She was wearing a brooch Vince hadn't seen before, a large dull blue stone; she kept fingering it as if to reassure herself she hadn't lost it.

The same shiny faced waiter brought them their drinks – juice for Vince and his granddad and his grandma's coffee. His grandfather looked worried.

"I thought you weren't allowed...," he said in a quavering voice.

"Oh Alfred," his grandma said, "it hardly matters *now*, does it?" But she didn't sound irritated like she normally did; she was smiling, and caught the eye of the young waiter and smiled even more. Vince was reminded of something but he couldn't think what.

"Grandma," he said suddenly, "how old *are* you?"

She paused mid-sip and looked at him over the top of her cup, and Vince wondered why he'd asked. He'd suddenly realised he didn't know how old either of his grandparents were, and it had seemed a stupid thing not to know.

But after a long pause his grandma told him, and emboldened he asked how old his granddad was too.

"Well Alfred?" his grandma said. "Your grandson asked you a question." But his granddad just looked perplexed; earlier he had seemed sharper, more like the joking old man Vince dimly remembered, but now he just looked baffled.

"How *old* am I?" he said, looking around the room.

"Hopeless," Vince's grandma muttered under her breath, then told Vince his age herself.

"So Granddad's older?" Vince said. "By five years?"

His grandma frowned.

"It's not how *long* you live Vince," she said, almost snapping as if he had got something wrong. "It's the quality of how you fill those years." Her face softened again; she fiddled with her brooch and spoke looking at Vince's granddad not Vince. "That's why this holiday is so important..."

But Vince was no longer listening, for he'd noticed Alice come into the dining room with her grandmother, who was hunched over a stick. Alice had black bags under her eyes, as if she hadn't slept at all (Vince had fallen asleep when the music had stopped just after midnight). His grandma noticed where Vince was looking.

"Probably a bit too old to be friends with you," she said in a cautious tone of voice. "Probably best not to get..."

"I've already *made* friends with her," Vince said, feeling annoyed with the old woman. "She's called Alice, she's nice."

His grandma looked over her shoulder at the two of them.

"Is she... Is it just her and her grandmother?" she said. "Not... just the *two* of them?"

"Yes," Vince said, "she has her own room too and... where are you going?" For his grandma had got up and was walking over to the young waiter; she had the look on her face she got when she was angry. Vince didn't understand why; adults just seemed to make up new things to get angry about whenever it suited them.

His grandfather hadn't noticed and was eating his fried breakfast in a clatter of cutlery; Vince couldn't hear the conversation between the waiter and his grandma properly, but he saw the smile never left the waiter's bland and greasy face.

"... will she pay?" Vince heard his grandma saying. She was gesturing over at where Alice and her grandma were sitting. The waiter appeared to be trying to say something placatory, but his grandma was still snapping. People were starting to notice.

"... ashamed!" the room heard her say. "A child!" Old faces turned up from their food in surprise; deaf voices asked each other what was happening.

Vince's granddad had stopped eating and looked upset. "Why is she shouting? What's happening?" he said with a mouthful of beans.

Vince looked back round for Alice, and saw she was already being hurried from the room by her grandmother. Alice looked somewhat shocked, and the small wave she gave to Vince was hesitant.

The young waiter stepped forward, and Vince saw an odd thing: although his grandma was still angry, she quavered and shrank back.

"This is in *no* one's best interests!" the waiter said loudly, as if to the room.

He speaks like someone older, Vince thought.

"Remember what this is; remember what you *agreed* to! There are no questions here, and no moral high-ground!" The waiter took Vince's grandma by the arm and escorted her back to their table surprisingly firmly; she looked shame-faced but still angry.

"Don't get too friendly with that girl," she said to Vince as she sat down, wincing, and she barely spoke for the rest of breakfast.

It was all very odd.

They were going on a trip that day, to visit some local tower from the top of which you could see ten counties or more – Vince was excited by the idea, and to be leaving the dusty old hotel and the small village that they'd already exhausted. He rushed to get ready, and was waiting in the hotel lobby for his grandparents, kicking his heels against the legs of the bench he was sitting on. He was hidden by a rack of leaflets and tourist maps; he didn't think the man behind the desk could see him. It was the same boy who'd been their waiter; his bland face not marked by the boredom he must be feeling. Did he spend *all* his time here? Vince had yet to see any other staff in the hotel at all.

The lift doors opened and two old ladies came slowly out, and hesitated as if nervous to approach the desk. They didn't look in Vince's direction, and seemed unaware of his presence. They looked identical to each other, and both wore the same thick coats and old-fashioned hats, although only one was carrying luggage. They must be checking out, Vince thought.

"Well...," one said quietly.

"Well...," the other said. "I guess it's time..."

"Yes," the first said, but they still didn't move. They weren't looking at each other as they spoke, but staring at the check-out desk. The boy must have noticed, but he busied himself with the pretence of tidying.

"Was it... worth it?" one of them said. Vince saw her reach out to take her sister's hand. They both looked on the verge of tears – old people are so weird! Vince thought.

"Oh yes!" the other said, smiling through her tears. "Oh yes... of course!" Smiling through her tears; like Comedy, Vince thought. For some reason he thought the old woman wasn't quite telling the truth, although he had no idea what they were talking about. He saw she was repeatedly squeezing her sister's hand.

"I wouldn't have wanted to go on *without* you," the other said doubtfully. "So as long as it was worth..."

"I won't be long behind you," the other said quickly. "Not with *this*." She gestured vaguely at her belly and grimaced.

The boy behind the desk cleared his throat, seemingly embarrassed. "Your taxi is here," he said.

The two women looked at each other. "Be brave," they both said to each other in the same tone, and then they smiled – genuine smiles this time, Vince thought. They embraced, and then without a word one them walked towards the hotel doors. So that's why all the tears, Vince thought, only one of them is going now. The sister who was leaving was struggling with her case; Vince noticed it wasn't shut properly, and something black and shimmery fell out. Vince couldn't tell what it was from where he was sitting, and didn't want to reveal his presence.

The lady who was left took a deep breath, shuddery with age. The smooth-faced boy came out from behind the desk to her. His face was shiny under the lights with the ointment he used. He briefly laid a hand on the old lady's shoulder – Vince couldn't tell if the mark it left was oily or dusty. He led her towards the wooden door at the back of the reception, the one with the carved faces.

"It's time," he said in a quiet voice.

The woman looked calmer now, resigned to something. The boy opened the wooden door and gestured her forward – ladies first. Why can't she just pay at the desk, Vince wondered. From where he was sat he couldn't see what was on the other side of the door. The old lady hesitated before entering.

"We both believe," she said, her voice still weak. "So I'll see her again..."

The boy was standing behind her, his hand on the base of her spine. Now he thought he was unobserved, the boy's blank, polite face cracked with an eager, almost mocking grin.

"Let's see," he said, and gently pushed her inside. He followed and shut the door behind them.

There was no noise, and they didn't come out again.

Eventually, bored, Vince scuttled forward. He picked up the object which had fallen from the first lady's case – he knew what he was doing was wrong, for without knowing what the soft, shiny black thing was he knew it was something *adult*, something rude even. But there was something nice about the way it felt, and he stuffed it guiltily into his pocket when he heard the lift doors open again.

"Come along then," his grandma said, as if *he* were the one who was late, "we haven't got all day." She shivered, and looked round the deserted lobby.

"Where are we going? Who is *he*?" his granddad said, and Vince realised with a shock his grandma was holding back tears. What was it about all the old people crying in this place?

"Where'd you get that?" Alice said.

Vince started guiltily, tried to hide the thing in his hands.

"It fell out a lady's suitcase," he said reluctantly.

The trip to the tower had not been a success – as soon as they'd started out from the hotel it had started to rain, and at the coach stop the three of them had all tried to huddle under his grandma's umbrella. And when they'd finally got to the tower they'd found out there was no way up it other than a narrow spiral staircase which neither of Vince's grandparents could manage. So he'd climbed it alone, the worn dusty steps seemingly too narrow even for his small feet, clutching the rope banister all the way up. And when he'd reached the top the day was so overcast and foggy he'd barely been able to see the county he was in, let alone all the other ones that were supposed to be visible. He'd been able to see his grandparents though, small figures waiting at the exit gate – his granddad kept trying to walk off and his grandma kept holding his arm to stop him doing so. Then he'd seen her convulse silently, hunch her shoulders – the first sneeze. All the way back on the coach she'd kept sneezing, glaring balefully at anyone who dared offer her a sympathetic glance. She'd gone straight to her room as soon they'd got back to the hotel, telling the fresh-faced boy behind the desk that she'd be better by the evening (although Vince didn't understand why *he* needed to know). His granddad had gone to their room too, and Vince was left to mope around the hotel, for the rain had turned torrential outside.

Alice sat down next to him on the bench. "You know what it *is* don't you?" she said. "It's a stocking."

Vince hadn't known the word, but nodded. He knew it was like half his mother's tights, but softer, prettier – naughty somehow, rather than practical.

"I didn't think all these old biddies still wore things like... *that*," Alice said, frowning. "This place is weird. I'm glad we're leaving tomorrow."

Vince felt faintly uneasy as he remembered the two old sisters he'd seen checking out that morning, but he didn't know how to articulate that unease to Alice. Didn't want, either, to admit to her that the whole hotel unnerved him slightly. He realised he was sitting so close to Alice that he could hold her hand, if he wanted to. He didn't know if he wanted to or not. He started to blush and felt angry with himself.

They told each other their birthdays; as he'd thought Alice was older than he was. They told each other where they lived, although neither lived in a place the other had heard of. They moaned about the boring hotel and village, which were both full of old people. They giggled about the way their grandparents smelt so musty, about their wrinkled hands reaching out blindly, about wrinkled old lips puckering up for a kiss on the cheek.

"She's not *really* my grandma you know," Alice said.

"What do you mean?"

"After *my* mum died my dad got married again," Alice said neutrally. "And then *she* died. But *her* mum, she still keeps coming round, and makes me call her Granny. I haven't got any real granny so I suppose it's alright. But I didn't want to come on holiday with her."

There were lots of different ways to respond to all of that and Vince didn't know which was best, so he grunted and kicked his legs against the bench. "I didn't want to come with mine," he said, although that wasn't strictly speaking true.

"Have you noticed you're the only people here where there are more than two of you?" Alice said and then counted on her fingers, "you, your granny, your grandda. Everyone else, there's just two of them. Weird."

"Weird," Vince said.

"Listen I've got to go," Alice said. "My granny makes me wash and change before dinner. I don't know why, we never go out. She's not my real granny," she added, almost as an afterthought. "Listen, if the music starts tonight will you meet me down here again?" She gestured around the empty lobby. "It's spooky on your own."

Vince nodded; she briefly squeezed his hand before she stood and ran clattering up the hotel stairs.

Vince paced his hotel room, feeling pent up and agitated. The sound of the rain against the window, and of the clock ticking, fought from either side of the room to annoy him. There was nothing to do in this stupid room, and it was cold too. He kept screwing up his nose as if to sneeze, but never doing so; maybe he'd caught what his grandma had. Bored, he pushed against the connecting door between his room and his grandparents' and was surprised when it gave – they'd obviously forgot to lock it their side. As soon as it had opened a fraction he could hear snoring – his grandfather's loud but somehow comforting snores, and his grandma's sniffy little ones, expressing disapproval even as she slept.

Cautiously, knowing he was doing wrong, Vince tiptoed in. The room was a larger version of his own. He was surprised that they had two separate beds, not a double like his parents. There was a clock ticking in this room too, but not in synch with his own (which he could still hear through the open door) so that the combined seconds of the two seemed to be passing double-time. There was a whole host of bottles of pills and medicines on the top of one chest of drawers, a leaflet called *Palliative Care: The Facts* – Vince didn't know what that was – and a box of earplugs.

The rain beat against the window with a fresh burst of vigour, so that the room was surprisingly noisy: the rain; the snores; the ticking seconds.

Not knowing why he was being so reckless, Vince opened one of the drawers – some musty smelling clothes, a dusty Bible. He shut it, opened a few other drawers, found nothing exciting. This is supposed to be a *holiday!* he thought. The sound of snoring hadn't even paused, so he listlessly opened one of the two wooden wardrobes.

These clothes didn't smell musty – there were long, luxurious looking dresses hung up, green and blue and gold. They were obviously old but well cared for. Vince didn't understand fashion or know much history, but he had the idea that these dresses were from when his granny (as Alice said) had been young, and she'd obviously treasured them all these years. But why bring them on holiday to this crummy dump? There were shoes neatly aligned below the dresses, and on a shelf to the side the brooch he'd seen her wearing the other day, and a pearl necklace. There were some shawls too, and Vince reached out to touch one – its smooth feel reminded him of the stocking he still had screwed up in his pocket.

Thinking about the stocking made him feel guilty, and *then* he felt guilty about snooping too. Just then his granny made a phlegmy sound as she snored, and turned her head restlessly. Quickly, Vince closed the wardrobe and hurried to his own room, shutting the connecting door gently behind him.

The rain died.

And so, unlike Alice and her granny, Vince and his grandparents did leave the hotel to eat that night – there was a fish and chip 'restaurant' on the open green where they could eat outside. The portions were huge and Vince and his granddad threw greasy scraps to the pigeons and jackdaws until his grandma told them to stop. But she didn't put as much force into it as she normally would; indeed she seemed distracted and fidgety, as if their meal was just a thing to be endured until something exciting came along, rather than the highlight of an evening where they'd go to bed before it was even fully dark.

"Still five nights to go," his grandma said, "and this one too of course." She smiled but was obviously thinking of somewhere else, for her smile didn't include Vince or his granddad. She seemed to realise she was being inattentive, for she suddenly smiled brightly at Vince. "Are you enjoying your holiday with your Grandma and Granddad?" she said.

"Yes Grandma," said Vince politely; then, because something more seemed to be required of him, "Maybe we could go on holiday together next year."

"Oh I should think so," his granddad said through a mouthful of chips.

"Vince I don't think..." his grandma said simultaneously. She frowned, looked at her hands. She had hardly eaten anything, Vince noticed, as if she were nervous or excited about something. "People the same age as your granddad and I... Well, things can happen suddenly. That's why I wanted to have this holiday *now*, just the three of us."

"Stop your prattle," his grandfather said, "I'm as fit as a fiddle. Of course the boy can come away with us again. Who did you say he was?"

Later they walked back by the river, where gnats hung like a shimmer across the path. Vince's grandfather told him gnats only lived for twenty-four hours, but Vince didn't know whether to believe him. "So they have to make hay while they can," his granddad said with a smile that somehow made what he'd said rude, although it wasn't (it didn't make *any* sense to Vince). He'd expected his grandma to be annoyed again, but she just said "Amen" under her breath, and only Vince heard.

He wondered if they'd be playing the same loud old music that night, and hoped that they would (whoever 'they' were) for then he'd be able to meet Alice downstairs again.

Vince was the quickest walker of the three, but this evening his grandma kept pace with him, seemingly impatient to get back to the hotel, and the ticking clock in her room (Vince felt *bored* already). His grandfather lingered behind, making quacking noises back at the ducks and throwing them chips.

"It's because of the war," his grandma said suddenly. "Rationing. He never likes to waste food, even if it gets eaten by birds." She paused, sniffing heavily. "Your granddad's not very well you know Vince."

"What do you mean?" Vince said, looking back. "I know his knees hurt and he can't always hear..."

"No, no, I mean... You can't always tell when people are sick, Vince. I... your granddad, you know he can't always remember your name..?"

"Oh I know old people forget things," Vince said airily.

"No... well yes. But he's not going to get *better*, your granddad, he's going to keep forgetting more and more things. Do you understand?"

Vince didn't meet her questioning gaze, for he felt his grandma (who he loved) was being shifty, was using adult justification for something she shouldn't be doing. Something he'd overheard his parents say when they thought he wasn't listening came to him, and he said it out loud – "Grandma are you going to put Granddad in a *home?*" – even though he didn't understand what it meant, or why 'home' was spoken about by his parents in a hushed voice like it was a bad thing rather than a good one.

"What? Certainly not," his grandma said primly, looking shocked, as if Vince had said a rude word. "No. We promised each other... He was *insistent*. That it would never come to that;

that if I'm not around to look after him... That's partly why... why this holiday."

"But you *are* around to look after him Grandma," Vince said. His grandmother seemed to snap out of whatever introspective thoughts she was having.

"Yes," she said. "Yes. But will you do your Grandma a favour tonight Vince?" He nodded. "Make sure you give your granddad a big, big hug goodnight. Promise me now."

Vince promised, feeling confused, and then they were back at the hotel. The greasy faced young man was *still* behind the front desk and he smiled at Vince's grandma as they entered.

The music started just after eleven o'clock – it *was* the same tune over and over again, Vince realised. He'd slept with his clothes on so he wouldn't feel so vulnerable outside as he had wearing pyjamas. Eagerly he got out of bed, opened the door to the hotel corridor – it was deserted and ghostly in the dusty light. Vince headed towards the hotel stairs, which spiralled down to the lobby.

Vince was surprised that despite his haste, Alice had beaten him. She looked bright eyed when she saw Vince, and anxious to tell him something.

"I came down here *before!*" she said excitedly into his ear. "I snuck down and I hid so I could be here before the music started. And guess what?"

"What?" said Vince, catching her excitement.

"People went in, old people from the hotel! That waiter man stood with the door open like he was greeting them, and they went in and when he shut it that's when the music started. My granny and yours!"

"My granny?" Vince said doubtfully. "But she's asleep upstairs, she needs her sleep..." Alice shook her head vigorously.

"That's what *my* granny says too but they both went in there!" she said, pointing to the heavy wooden door, with its twin carved faces.

"What about my granddad?" Vince said.

"No not him," Alice said. "It was weird, but for all the granny and granddas here, only *one* of each went in. Like only one was allowed."

They stood for a minute in the dull darkness of the hotel reception, neither speaking. The same tune was still repeating itself, muffled by the door. Alice hugged herself; Vince wondered if he should hug her to warm her up, but he didn't dare. For some reason his heartbeat was up and audible to him, like the ticking of those annoying clocks.

"Shall we *open* it?" Alice said. Vince gawped. "Just a *peek?* It's my last night, how else will I find out what's going on? Just a peek Vince, *please?*" One look at her bright eyes and Vince realised he was going to say yes to her, despite the nervous dizziness in his stomach.

They went up to the old door with its grinning faces – the dull light played tricks and they both looked like Comedy. The music was still playing the repetitive tick-tock tune, and it still sounded like it was coming from both just the other side of the door and a long, long way away.

It'll be locked, Vince thought as Alice reached out for the doorknob, it won't open... But it turned easily in her hand, and with some effort the two of them opened the heavy door.

It opened onto stone steps, spiralling down into what was presumably a cellar or basement; the steps were worn and dusty. There were footsteps in the dust, but already partially obscured; how could there be so much dust *already?* Vince thought. His nose tickled.

There was a glow of light coming up the stairs, and oddly the music sounded quieter now they'd opened the door, and less muffled. It was a different tune too, Vince realised, he must have been mistaken before.

"Shall we go *down?*" Alice breathed in his ear, sounding excited. She's holding my hand, Vince thought, how long has she been holding my hand? He felt giddy and sick, and knew he wasn't going to refuse her. They both took their shoes off, to be quieter.

Tip-toeing, holding hands, they cautiously descended the staircase. Alice screwed up her face as her bare feet touched the dusty stone. There was a rusty iron banister which Vince clung to as they descended; it was loose and moved in his hand. Dust hung in the air, seemed to fall from the ceiling and walls, and catch in the back of Vince's throat.

About half-way down they found a comb that looked like it had been dropped by someone; it was already half-covered in dust. Alice picked it up; it had a few grey hairs entangled in it. "Weird," she mouthed, dropping it. She wiped her hand on her dress.

They froze at the bottom of the stairs; there was no door, the stairs just opened out into a large room, which was lit by lamps and candles. Vince and Alice crouched down just outside the circle of light but could see almost the entire room. Tables had been pushed up to the walls to clear the middle; on one side the tables had been laid with a whole range of delicious and exotic looking food; on the other stood twinkling glasses and lots of different bottles of alcohol. There were also packets of cigarettes and boxes of cigars, and a gramophone, from which the music still played.

And the room was full of young people.

Their young forms were smooth and soft in the candlelight, and most were dancing elegantly in the centre of the room. The men wore spotless evening suits, crisp black and white except for notes of individual colour – a scarlet cummerbund, a crimson bow-tie, a blood red rose at a lapel. The women all wore long, flowing dresses, and although Vince knew nothing about fashion, when he heard Alice gasp in admiration he couldn't mock her for being a girl, for even he could see that none of these women would ever wear a dress that suited them *this* well again... Some wore the fur of dead animals around their shoulders; some wore long feathers in their hair, which caught in the light as they danced with the men. In the background of discrete shadows one of the couples had stopped dancing, and the young lady had her leg raised up to be grasped by the man's squeezing hand; her thigh was the same soft black colour as the stocking screwed up in Vince's pocket...

Vince felt the tickle of dust in his nose and throat again, which was odd, for down *here* there was no dust; everything was clean and fresh and new looking.

The record playing on the gramophone came to an end and a man moved over to change it – Vince recognised the young lad who was seemingly the hotel's only employee; for once his face seemed devoid of the greasy residue of whatever ointment he used on it. His shining shoes clacked against the smooth wooden floor as he moved to the gramophone, and in the gap in the music people changed partners on the dance floor. Priority was given to those who had stood this dance aside – all seemed amicable. Even the kissing couple in the shadows separated, the woman to be kissed by a different man, the original gentleman to examine the cigars, one of which he lit and smoked with as much relish as he had stroked the woman's thigh seconds before. Then the music started again, and all the couples began dancing...

Vince rubbed his nose to try and stifle a sneeze.

"Oh shall we *dance?*" Alice whispered in his ear. "Do you think they'd mind?" No one had noticed the two of them yet. But they all looked so kindly and good that Vince didn't think they would mind or tell them off or send them to their beds. But *he* dance, with a girl! He had the usual scorn of a boy his age at the notion, and yet beneath these automatic thoughts was the idea that yes, he could; she was holding his hand and he could dance with her to this lilting music, in the candlelight and exotic smelling cigar smoke. Vince found himself tensing to step forward and lead Alice by the hand onto the dance floor...

He didn't meet the lady's eyes, for he was still too nervous to want to draw attention to himself, but he saw the sparkle of a brooch on her dress, the string of pearls around her throat. She was young and very pretty, Vince thought, pretty like Alice was with a soft, rounded face. She wore a long blue dress, a soft blue that suited her, as did her muted red lipstick and...

"That lady's stolen my granny's brooch!" Vince shouted. And her necklace. He had stepped out into the light of the room without realising it, and was pointing an accusing finger at the woman; he'd let go of Alice's hand and had left her in the shadows, from where he heard her gasp as he spoke. He felt shockingly indignant – the brooch was so distinctive there could be no mistake, and this woman who looked so fresh and pretty and danced so nicely had *stolen* it. Vince was aware of Alice coming forward to his side, and he wondered if she'd be mad at him for ruining things, but she took his hand like before.

Everyone in the room had stopped dancing or eating or kissing or drinking and turned to stare at Vince. They looked shocked – speechless rather than angry. The woman he'd accused tried to speak but didn't seem to know what to say; her face had flushed prettily with anger or guilt. Then she ducked behind some of the other young people, as if wanting to hide herself from Vince...

Then Vince heard Alice take a little intake of breath; she took her hand from his and pointed accusingly at one of the ladies too – a different one; the one who had been in the shadows and kissing so many of the men...

"*Granny?*" Alice said.

Vince turned to gawp at her – why was she calling someone so young her *granny?* He was about to say something when the lingering sensation of dusty air made him sneeze; his eyes closed and filled with tears as if to wash away the non-existent irritant of the dust...

He opened his eyes and everything looked different.

It was just the basement of the hotel, lit by weak and flickering electric lighting that was strung unsafely from the crumbling plaster ceiling. The floor people were dancing on was unswept bare boards, thick with dust (bits of dead people, Vince thought). At the edge of the room there was food on rickety tables; plates green with age and mould. The drink bottles looked cloudy and stagnant. There was a record player but its needle scratched and slipped across the disk, creating an arrhythmic and discordant ticking sound.

And the room was full of old people.

Vacant and wrinkled looking faces stared at Vince, their mouths hung open, their eyesight not reaching him; bodies bent over, wearing old clothes that no longer fitted their figures – either too tight over their bloating, or too big hanging from their fatless bodies. One lady had stockings curled like dead skin down to her knees; one man's dentureless mouth was clasped tight round an unlit and spittle-wet cigar like it was a dummy. Clumsy feet shuffled in time to a beat Vince could no longer hear (there was none in the discordant scratching that played now); hems of dresses and faded suit trousers brushed against the dust.

And despite their age, Vince could feel the seething of their emotions like an electric hum in the room: the jealousy when the person with whom they wished to dance danced with another; the shame and pettiness of their lust for drink and narcotics and each other; their desperation not to be left to one side of the room, not to be the one who did the stupid thing or spoke out of turn. They weren't even *enjoying* what they'd come here to do, and they couldn't even admit they weren't enjoying it.

"What are *you two* doing here?" – the young waiter moved in front of Vince, blocking his view of the old people before he'd had a chance to properly take it all in. *He* still looked young, although his face was all greasy again, Vince saw; the grease almost coating his face, his hands too, and it made him look grey and sick, for it was studded from all the endless dust which fell from the ceiling and swirled from the floor.

Vince tried to answer, but his throat was still itchy and his nose ticklish, and he closed his eyes and sneezed again...

When he reopened his eyes everything was back to how it had been just seconds before – the room full of young people and his finger still pointing at the pretty thief of his grandma's jewellery; Alice still incomprehensibly accusing some youthful stranger of being her granny.

"What are you doing here?" the young boy was still saying. His face no longer looked grey with dust but it seemed pulled taut with anger, stretched over something livid beneath. He seemed barely in control of himself as he span round to look at everyone else in the room; they shrank from his gaze. "You all know the *rules*," he said accusingly to the crowd, then he seemed to tremble as he controlled himself, spoke in a more measured tone. "Did either of you two tell them about... this?" he said.

He looked in turn to the woman who had stolen the brooch, and the one Alice had called 'granny'.

"No, no," they said from opposite sides of the room, in fluttery voices that didn't seem to fit their fresh and youthful aspects.

Everyone was staring at the seething, twitching young waiter, as if he wasn't the one who took orders but the one who gave them. He was sweating now, and Vince noticed his sweat cut a path through the grease on his face; his skin didn't seem the same colour underneath.

"Well," he said, "well. You'll have to leave early of course. And *pay* early."

The atmosphere in the room changed, although Vince struggled to understand exactly how. It didn't make sense; these people weren't even staying at the hotel! The young jewellery thief was dabbing her eyes with an old-fashioned lace handkerchief; Vince recognised the handkerchief too.

The other lady seemed more composed; she smoothed her dark green dress and walked towards Alice. Her pretty face now seemed another creation of makeup and ointment; Vince wanted to sneeze again. He wanted to run out the basement and up the stairs, but now these grownups had spotted them both he and Alice had lost all volition.

Alice clasped his hand again, was leaning to whisper something in his ear... but the lady in the green dress rudely pulled her away. Alice's fingers slipped through his like someone falling.

"Granny?" Alice said tremulously to the lady who was leading her away, who couldn't be more than twenty-one. There was a muttering around the room – "for shame!" one of the young men said quietly. But no one moved. All Vince could think was that he didn't want to get told off; he felt confused and close to tears.

"Granny!" Alice said in pain as the woman yanked at her arm again; she was pulling Alice across to where the waiter stood.

"As you've so often reminded me you ungrateful brat," the woman said, "I'm *not* your granny."

Alice looked back at Vince as if appealing for him to do something, but he didn't know what and so he did nothing.

"Perfect," the hotel boy said as he laid a hand on Alice's shoulder. She stopped pulling away at his touch, and when he let go she stood stock still with her back to Vince. He saw a greasy mark on her dress where the boy's hand had been.

"And you?" the boy said to the lady wearing the stolen brooch. She was still in tears and didn't respond; the boy shrugged and walked towards Vince, leaving Alice motionless in the same statue-like pose. He was grinning and had tracks of grey scored through his greasy face.

"Wait! No!" the lady he'd addressed cried out, snapping from her thoughts. "Not... for mercy's sake! My husband will pay!" She looked round the room as if seeking approval. "At the end of my week... He'd got... He's not got his wits, he..."

The young waiter had paused at her words, and only Vince had seen the look of hatred that had passed across his face as she had spoke. He looked cowed into taking orders again. He turned to face her.

"But he can't *stay*. For a week? What if he comes down again? What if he tells..."

"He's just a *child*," the lady interrupted. The boy angrily ran a hand through his hair, left it dishevelled with the greasy ointment he smeared through it. He glanced at Alice (who still hadn't moved since he'd laid his hand on her) and this seemed to calm him somewhat.

"Either that," he said, "or you all three leave early. No payment but get out. He's a risk..."

"But I'm here for the whole week!" the lady interrupted, and the fearless way she did so remind Vince of something, although he couldn't have said what. "This is my last..."

"I will not be swayed in this," the boy said. He glanced towards Alice again, his eyes eager with something.

Turn around, Vince was thinking – if she'd just turn and ask him to do something then he *would*, but without her asking him he didn't know what...

And then the lady with the brooch had him by the arm and was dragging him towards the spiral stairs that led up to the hotel lobby. The music started up again as if a vast distance away, and the young people started dancing. The shapes they made together were beautiful and blocked Vince's view of Alice.

"But she's stolen my grandma's brooch!" he cried out to them.

"Oh for heaven's sake *Vince!*" the young lady snapped.

The next morning Vince supposed it must all have been a dream. Well not all of it; he'd probably fallen asleep in the hotel lobby and dreamt the rest, and Alice had somehow got him back to his room. Or maybe the dream had started later than that, for he did have dust on his clothes, and the taste of it in the back of his mouth.

Earlier than he expected his grandma came through the connecting door between the two rooms.

"Pack your bags, Vince," she said, "we're leaving."

"But we've got all week!" he protested.

"It's... your grandfather," she said. "He's sick." She muttered something else under her breath as she turned away.

"But we can come again next year, right?" Vince said,

"Vince! Pack!" his granny shouted. Vince didn't understand why, if she was so angry, she also seemed to be crying too.

But she's got her brooch on, he thought. So it *had* to have been a bad dream, after all.

The hotel lobby was empty; it was so early the young boy was still being a waiter in the dining room rather than manning the desk. There was a bell to ring for attention, but his grandma didn't press it. She seemed eager to leave, she shooed Vince and his grandfather towards the door.

Outside was not one but two taxis.

"Grandma we haven't *paid*," Vince said. He was trying to look through the frosted glass door to the dining room to see Alice one last time.

"We don't have to," his grandma said. "Because, well, we're leaving so early. Lucky for your grandfather they let us off..."

"Where *are* we?" the old man said in a weak voice. Vince's grandma set her lips in a thin tight line.

They got into one of the waiting taxis outside; Vince sneezed and his grandma gave him a tissue to blow his nose. As they were pulling away Vince stared out the back window of the cab to get one last look at the hotel.

An old lady, wincing and looking like she had been crying, was getting into the other taxi. She struggled with her luggage until the driver got out to help her.

Alice, thought Vince, for it was Alice's grandmother.

But the old lady got into the back of the taxi on her own, shut the door, and then it too pulled away, in the opposite direction.

THE MAN DOGS HATED

You could always tell when he was out walking in the neighbourhood, because you'd hear the dogs barking all along his route. He walked most evenings, that was one of the things about him. I'd be sitting having a glass of wine with Deborah on the patio – the sun would just be sinking and the evening would have that clear, golden quality to it. And then the peace would be broken by barking, or even howling, as *he* passed a dog-owner's house somewhere – it made you shiver, a bit, to hear that wolf-like howling across the English summer.

Deborah would look at me like she expected me to *do* something, but I'd just gesture her inside. She didn't understand it wasn't for me to act unilaterally; things don't work like that here.

What was worse was when he passed a dog in the street. I saw it happen a few times. He'd just be standing there, whilst the dog-walker tried to drag their mutt away. And the dog would be snarling and slobbering and straining on its lead to *get* to him. They weren't scared of him, it seemed more like intrinsic hatred. Even the most placid of pets, even old Bob's blind-dog, would go feral at the sight of him – the smell of him maybe. You know when dogs bare their teeth and you realise how *animal* they are? Not cuddly pets at all but beasts.

I'm not a dog person, myself.

And *he* just stood there and the odd thing was he looked at them with such affection, almost simple-looking – a man who loved dogs. They wanted to tear his throat out and he just grinned like a fool in love. Maybe he was simple? It would explain a lot. But I never forget that look in his eyes. That look was why I didn't believe the stories that he killed dogs, poisoned pets. Not *those* stories, no. And events proved me right on that one.

It makes me wonder if some of the other stories about him weren't falsehoods too: him being near that playground; the strange noises from his house at night; him just standing staring at people through shop windows like he didn't realise they could see him too. Not that it makes much difference what was true and what wasn't. He *was* odd, no question, so we would have done the same as we did regardless of the specifics. We were all agreed on *that*. You can't be too careful, in a neighbourhood like this one.

I've lived here for close to twenty years now; I still remember when we first arrived, Deborah and I, and how it immediately felt like *home*. Not our new house, not being married, but the place itself, the neighbourhood. Felt like the place I'd been aiming for all my life, the place that finally made sense of all those late nights in the office, all that schmoozing with bosses I hated. The broad streets were lined with trees – old trees, as old as the houses perhaps. Newly washed cars glinting in the sun on long, curved drives. Every house set back from the road by a large and immaculate front lawn. I remember my father saying once that front lawns were pointless; they couldn't be used, he said, they were only for show, only for other people. I thought, *exactly*. I didn't want to live in the kind of street my father had lived in.

I felt like I'd arrived.

I wondered at the time whether there'd be a price for living somewhere like this, for belonging here as much as I did. It was McFarlane who showed me that there was.

He lived alone, in the old Anderson house – we still called it that, despite the fact that the Mievilles had lived there in the interim. The Mievilles had arrived with three children, so we could see why they'd bought a big old house like that despite not really being able to afford it, as it later transpired. The Mievilles had been welcomed into the neighbourhood initially; we weren't prejudiced or anything. How a man makes his money is his own business. And we were glad someone was going to do up the old Anderson place, which was an eyesore and was starting to drag down prices for the whole street. But the Mievilles didn't do it up at all, they just left it to get worse. If they couldn't afford it they shouldn't have moved in. We were friendly enough telling them that it wasn't on, at first. And there was no prejudice, as I say.

How *he* could afford the house no one knew. He certainly didn't go to work. The postman told us he received a lot of mail, cheques he thought. From where or whom we never knew. We didn't even know *how* he'd bought the house – not through Havershaw and McFarlane like everyone else does around here. So McFarlane disliked him from the off, but that isn't to say he wasn't given a fair chance.

People thought he was odd from the start, of course, but eccentric is allowed. (Think of Mrs Needham and all her damn trinkets; think of old Bob obsessively polishing his medals, though we all know he gets them from car boot sales.) And he kept to himself, you had to give him that much. Never spoke to you unless you spoke to him first, and even then you rarely got more than a goofy smile in response. If you made gestures when speaking he stared at your hands not your face. You could tell he was odd, not eccentric but *odd*, as soon as you saw him. In the same way I knew I belonged here, all those years ago, I knew he didn't. Against the trim lawns and discrete houses he looked wrong, walking around grinning, in ill matching clothes. He stood out. He mismatched.

We gave him a chance but he never... He didn't fix his garden up, didn't repair the old Anderson place. Nor did he attend neighbourhood fetes or functions. Never applied to join the golf club or the Rotary. These things take up time, I know, but sacrifices have to be made in a place like this.

And gradually the rumours started about him; I don't know how many were actually true: he'd been seen on the school playing field late at night; he spent an unusually long time in the WCs at the library; he *never* put out any rubbish for the bin men on Tuesdays.

"You'll never guess what I heard about that man today..!" Deborah would say to me, and I never asked her who she had heard her stories *from*.

I know a few of the rumours were true: how he'd taken a cake Angie Havershaw had bought round as a welcome gift and put it straight out in his garden for the birds. I could see him from my bedroom window, standing amid all the squabbling crows and pigeons. Like I say, just odd – I mean Angie can't cook for toffee we all know that, but there are some things that you just don't do.

The stories kept piling up about him; whether each specific tale was true I don't know, but the sum total of them was. He would have to leave, just like it was made clear to the Mievilles, after it became obvious.

McFarlane called, and said it was time.

~

Now that I think about it, despite all his oddness I think it was those damn dogs that did for him, in the end. Their constant howling across our streets, unable to get rid of their hatred.

When McFarlane made it clear we were welcome here, truly welcome here, with his clap on the back and proffered brandy in the golf club bar, it felt like an initiation, a ritual indicating a test passed. Of course, I'd heard the stories about him by then, roguish lech that he was… but like I say eccentric is allowed. I sipped the brandy and toasted him ironically. It's an easy memory to recover, because the golf club bar hasn't changed in all these years, and neither has McFarlane.

"Welcome to the neighbourhood," he said. "I do hope I'm going to get to meet your good wife at some point?" and I made a mental note to invite him round, despite the anxiety I knew Deborah always felt entertaining strangers. "So nice," he'd continued, "to have the *right* kind of people in the neighbourhood. Not like that new couple just moved in on Victoria road…" He trailed off, and let me say the rest.

They were the first, that I was involved in.

The evening we went to speak to him, the man the dogs hated, I stepped out the front door, and already a dog was barking somewhere. McFarlane's way of making people who didn't fit in leave was simplicity itself – it was meant to be just a gentlemanly chat. Business-like – and this *was* business, of a kind. We would explain that there were places for people like us, and places for people like him, and those two sets of places didn't always overlap. In his case certainly didn't. Sometimes when we spoke to people they were even half-relieved, because the situation was surely obvious to them too. Sometimes they didn't take much persuading. And if they did, well, there were other ways.

There were about ten of us that night, more than normal. I had almost not gone, but I'd remembered Deborah's scornful look every time I'd ushered her inside the shadowy house from the patio when the howling started, and I changed my mind.

Rather than knocking on his door, we decided it best to confront him when he was on one of his odd evening walks. He had no set route but we just headed towards the sound of barking. There was a sense of camaraderie on these occasions, a sense of shared purpose. But I don't mind admitting that feeling was strained that night; it was almost spooky, to be out walking at sunset and hear all those dogs howling and yapping at the sky. I felt a little nervous. I hadn't with the Mievilles, hadn't for years, but I did that night.

We saw his shadow first, stretched and black in the sunset. It moved with the same aimlessness that he did – like he owned the place. But he was surprisingly fast for that, and before we could stop him he turned up Goose Gate, which was a cul-de-sac (so why go up there?) and so we decided to wait at the bottom of the street for him to come back down. For a moment it was peaceful – the only sound the swifts screeching. Then there was a commotion – we walked up a bit to look. The newcomers at Number 20 had let their dog roam loose in their garden and it was up on its hind legs at the fence, barking like it thought it was three times bigger than it was. All we could see of him was his silhouette, which paused, like it wanted to go and befriend the thing despite the hatred in its bark. Then he slowly turned and walked back down the street, towards where we were waiting.

I'll never know whether he actually understood what we had to say to him. Oh he nodded, and said yes a few times, but his eyes still had that glazed, simple look, so who could tell? He frowned at some things, not in anger but like he didn't understand the concept at all – didn't understand housing equity or why he shouldn't talk to children. It was mostly like he heard our words but didn't grasp their import (like Angie said, maybe he *was* foreign, despite the flat accent). When he looked between us it was always a few seconds after one of us had stopped speaking and the other started.

But then his eyes lit up; he was smiling but not at us. He was looking at something behind us.

I turned to look – Mrs Douglas was slowly walking along the main street, towards the turn off to Goose Gate. She had that small yappy poodle trotting along on a lead. She called it Precious, of all things, and it had always been a noisy and cantankerous dog even before *he* had come here. It hadn't seen him yet, it was lingering behind to sniff at some piss on a lamppost; Mrs Douglas was carrying a small freezer bag with its crap in it. Better than when it had used to lie in the street, but my nose still wrinkled with distaste. I don't know who's worse, dogs or their owners.

We called out to her to stay on the opposite side of the road, so she could walk Precious past without too much uproar when it noticed *him*. But she couldn't hear us. Instead the deaf old idiot started crossing the street to try and hear what we were saying. We gestured at her to go back, and she stopped in the middle of the road in confusion.

Precious had noticed by now, and was barking and straining at its lead. The thing looked *rabid*. I thought that it must just sense that he's not right, in some way, like we did.

Get back, we said again, but she walked forward instead.

Just then two bikes came down the main street – just kids racing. Our roads are pretty quiet, so children are safe on bikes. One went one side of Mrs Douglas, one the other, and they were laughing and hollering; one reached out to tap Mrs Douglas on the shoulder as he passed – a childhood prank that made me nostalgic. It was *nothing*; but Mrs Douglas reacted like she'd been shot. She cried out, threw both her hands up in the air, staggered back a few steps. The boys went giggling off into the night; the freezer bag of dog shit flew into the air; and Precious was suddenly racing across the road snarling, lead clattering behind it. Its teeth were bared and its eyes bulged. We were all so startled we stepped back from the vicious looking thing.

I thought it was going to rip his throat out.

Of course, a small dog like that couldn't have done him much harm normally, despite how frenzied it looked. But the damn idiot bent down to it as it came, as if to pet it, as if to scoop it into a hug. He had that idiot look of affection in his eyes; his smile was wide and beatific.

Precious leapt...

The bag of shit fell back into our street and burst.

... the dog's forepaws caught him in his chest, his arms clasped the slavering dog in an embrace, and he fell backward with the impact...

Then there was one of those seconds which seemed much longer, or like you've blacked out, because everything was different afterwards.

He was lying on the pavement and Precious was stood atop him – at first I thought she was biting his face but she was just licking it. Her tail was wagging frantically and he had one hand up, just stroking her back and behind her ears. His eyes were closed.

No one knew what to do for a second – McFarlane was no bloody use – so I approached cautiously (it wasn't seemly, for him to be lying in the street as he was). I reached out for the lead, being careful not to touch the damn mutt itself, and the thing turned and growled at me with slobbering jaws. It looked at me with the hatred of dogs.

Then it turned back to him, all eager and affectionate again.

"Precious?" Mrs Douglas said weakly.

I reached out for the lead again, annoyed now. Precious turned and with no preamble, bit me in the hand.

I yelled out and stepped back; I turned to McFarlane to say something...

He was staring past me. "Look at *him*," he said.

The man had one hand against the pavement, and it was twitching. His eyes were closed and he was still smiling that smile, but his face looked grey and drained of blood. His chest was heaving up and down with slow, shuddering breaths; Precious rode up and down on it, still licking him with frantic affection. He still had one hand on the dog's back, no longer stroking but just as if to hold her in place.

"Your dog bit my bloody hand," I said to Mrs Douglas.

He died in front of us with no one moving, and then Precious stood on his chest and howled. After a few seconds there was another howl from Number 20. And then the sound was taken up by all the dogs of our neighbourhood – barking and howling into the empty night sky.

The family who have moved into the old Anderson place seem much more acceptable – he was in finance and we know a few of the same people. They have already started doing the place up. Mind you, they should be able to afford to do so; McFarlane says they got the place for a song because no one round here wanted it. And his wife has got to know my wife, I think. It's hard to say, because Deborah is staying with McFarlane, until the papers come through and we can sell the house.

I wonder how long it's been going on.

I could afford to buy her out and stay here, and indeed have been angrily telling people that I will. That this is *my* neighbourhood as much as hers. And people at the club, or in the street, or at the Rotary fete, say yes of course you must. And then they change the subject.

I don't know why Deborah reacted like she did – who made her judge of everyone all of a sudden? And after all McFarlane and the others were there *too*. Why do they still get slaps on the back at the clubhouse? Why do they still get invites to dinner, and Angie's inedible cakes, and compliments on their lawns?

Precious had to be put down of course. Technically there was no evidence that she contributed to his death (which is still officially "unexplained") but my testimony that she bit me did for her. So I can understand why Mrs Douglas dislikes me so, but not everyone else.

I can't say I'm upset about Precious. As I say, I've never really been a dog person.

And maybe the feeling is mutual, for when I go out for a walk in the evenings (it helps me to think through my feelings about the whole Deborah thing, if I am walking) I swear that they have all started barking at *me*.

SICK LEAVE

Emma entered the classroom and the children's conversation died instantly – they knew they were supposed to wait quietly for their teachers and they sat still and acted like they had. Emma had never before been so aware of this routine deception at the start of each day. She guessed it was because she had been off sick; she'd become unfamiliar with how things were in her absence. In a few days it would all seem normal again. She was aware of the children watching her as she put down her bag, smoothed her skirt, and sat at her desk at the front of the class. She started to greet them but sneezed instead; she turned away from the children to blow her nose and heard one of them say something that caused an outbreak of suppressed giggles.

"Hello class," she said eventually. "It's nice to see you all again after such a long time away."

"Hello, Miss Anderson," the seven year olds chorused raggedly. They all seemed different somehow: a haircut here, a lost tooth there, different clothes and different groups of friends. Emma couldn't help thinking that they'd all grown up in some significant yet subtle way.

"Are you better now, Miss?" Jo Webster asked out of the blue.

"Yes I'm fine, thank you for asking," Emma said. It was something of a lie, for her throat and sinuses still hurt, and her head still felt tired and flushed out. But she was over the worst of it, she was on the mend. Maybe she'd come back to work slightly too early but this was her first ever class. Emma was only twenty-three, and having got a full-time teaching job with implausible speed after qualifying she was both excited about it and terrified of screwing the whole thing up. Late at night she was kept awake by imagined mistakes and how their consequences could affect entire lives.

"What did you have, Miss?" Michael Potts said. "What disease?" They *had* grown in confidence, hadn't they? Michael Potts had used to be as quiet as a mouse in class. Emma shook her head, trying to shake off some of the tired fuzziness before answering.

"Just a touch of flu," she said. That was partly untrue as well, because no one had been quite sure *what* she'd caught. Some kind of super-flu probably, one of those antibiotic resistant strains that would be quite worrying if she allowed herself to think of them. Whatever it had been it had certainly knocked her off her feet, and she hadn't quite recovered yet. But lying in a sick bed remembering the past was not how Emma wanted to spend her time.

Michael didn't acknowledge Emma's reply but just stared at her. Leah, sitting next to him (when had those two become friends?) whispered something in his ear that made him smile. He didn't giggle and clamp a hand over his mouth, he didn't look at Leah and grin. He just sat there, smiling faintly, his bright eyes watching Emma.

She asked the children what they'd learnt from the supply teacher whilst she'd been off sick; their response was muted and unenthusiastic. Eventually Emma dragged it from them: the spellings they'd learnt, the sums they'd done, the Mother's Day cards they had made. The children seemed sullen and wary, glancing at each other before answering – it was a far cry from the lively and friendly class she'd used to teach, and Emma couldn't help but feel miserable. Her head throbbed painfully and she found it hard to smile.

"Anything else?" she said. "You must have learnt something else?"

Kevin Rhodes said something under his breath; somewhat more harshly than normal Emma asked him to repeat it.

"Black Death," the boy said reluctantly.

"The *plague*," another child said, with odd emphasis. The children looked at Emma with solemn starring eyes.

"O... oh?" Emma said, unsure what to make of this answer. Was the Black Death really on the curriculum for seven year olds? She would have to check; she didn't like to think that the supply teacher might have been teaching her class something inappropriate. "So what did you learn about it?" she asked, expecting answers about rats, fleas, and the Middle Ages.

The children glanced at each other. A few whispered something to their neighbours but not in any way that suggested a joke. Emma felt a wave of dizziness and put her hand against her desk to steady herself. She closed her eyes for a second, and as she did so Carl Burke started speaking:

"The bubonic plague is caused by a bacteria with a inoc... inoculation period of two to ten days. After that the vic... victim suffers fevers, swollen glands particularly in the groin, pro... prostration and delirium. There's a ninety percent chance of death."

Emma opened her eyes and stared at the boy. He'd said the words blankly, as if learnt by rote. All the children were watching her and she knew she should say something, but she wasn't quite sure how to respond. Had the supply teacher really taught her children such graphic details, or had Carl simply looked it up on the internet for some reason?

Before she could speak the classroom door opened and the head teacher, Mr Hall, entered. His smile looked painted onto his bald-egg face. Emma knew he didn't like her, knew he felt he and his school had been lumbered with someone too young to teach. She didn't feel she had done anything to deserve his dislike, but he always seemed to try and find fault with her.

"Ah, Miss Anderson," he said (he called all the other women teachers 'Ms.'). "Welcome back. I hope you're feeling better after your absence. Ah, flu wasn't it?"

"Yes," Emma said, looking away from Carl Burke. She was aware how petty and trivial 'flu' sounded when Mr Hall said it, as if she was a child who he'd caught skiving off., She was caught by surprise by another loud sneeze.

There was the low sound of the children starting to whisper again, and before Emma could react Mr Hall was yelling.

"Quiet! Miss Anderson and I are trying to talk!"

She felt angry, as she always did when someone else gave orders to *her* class. Mr Hall was always doing this, as if he thought she couldn't cope. The children went dumb instantly, and Mr Hall's next words seemed too loud in the new silence.

"Well, I was just checking you were, ah, better," he said to her. "You are sure you're well enough again now?"

"Fine," said Emma tightly, furious that he was daring question her in front of her class. For a moment she thought she was going to sneeze again, but she wrinkled her nose and fought it off.

"Ah," Mr Hall said; then, as if this were some kind of farewell, he left.

Emma turned back to her class; their faces blurred and wavered in her tired vision. She would need to have some more coffee during the break, despite wanting to cut down. She wondered whether to speak to Carl again, to find out where he'd learnt such gruesome facts ("particularly in the groin" her mind whispered) – not in class surely? But she decided to let the matter drop. Emma was thankful when the bell rang for the morning break, and her children ran out enthusiastically to the playground. "Walk!" she shouted, as she always did, and they ignored her, as they always did. This return to something like normal behaviour made her feel slightly better as she walked toward the staff room. Still, something else was nagging at her about what Carl Burke has said, and it took her awhile to work out what it was: the boy had spoken in the present tense.

Emma's heart sank as she entered the staff room and saw the rota – they had put her on playground duty. Outside it was a bleak, characterless day, not quite spring yet, but not really winter anymore either. It was just a cold, misty March day, the ground fog more substantial than the things it cloaked. Emma stood wrapped up in her coat and scarf, clutching a mug of coffee in both hands, its steam escaping into the quiet air. She thought of the other teachers in the warmth inside; they must have put her on the rota for today as soon as they'd known she was back, in revenge for having to cover for her whilst she'd been off sick.

The children screamed and scattered across a stretch of grey tarmac that was supposedly a playground. In one corner a steel spider's leg climbing frame was roped off, because of rust. The children compensated by playing tig, or British Bulldog, or a game of their own devising simply called 'War'.

Emma didn't notice at first, but the children from her class weren't running around or dying theatrical, bullet-ridden deaths. Instead they had ducked under the rope, and were stood in a clump under the corpse of the climbing frame at the far end of the playground. From what she could see all of her class were there, and no one else. Emma thought it odd – they all had friends in other classes, they all had antagonists in their own – so why were they suddenly such an exclusive group? They didn't even appear to be playing, they just seemed to be discussing or deciding something, very serious and adult-like in their oversized sweaters and "you'll grow into it" coats. Emma wanted to go and see what they were up to, but she had to deal with a boy from another class first, so far the only casualty of 'War'. The boy had grazed his knee when an enemy grenade had landed at his feet, and his loud snivelling hurt Emma's head. Using a tissue she wiped a slug-track of snot from his upper lip, and trembled in distaste.

When she'd dealt with the boy she was relieved to see her class were actually playing now. It seemed to soothe her slightly to see them, hand in hand in the mist, moving round in a circle, singing something childish and possibly rude. She waited for the circle to convulse with giggles as someone tripped or the naughty word was reached...

But nothing of the sort happened. Emma walked towards her class, and noticed how slowly and solemnly the children were playing. The look on their faces suggested they didn't want to be doing what they were doing, but knew they had to, liked adults performing a distasteful but essential task. As Emma got closer she could hear what they were singing; she remembered singing similar words herself:

"Ring around the rosie,

"A pocketful of posies,

"Ashes, ashes,

"We all fall down."

The words were being sung with no sense of pleasure, much like the children sang the dirge-like hymns Mr Hall selected for assembly. But this singing also seemed tense, fearful even, and Emma felt herself grew tense again too. The children didn't even fall down when they reached the final words, which from a kid's perspective was surely the best part?

When Emma was a few metres away from the circle it stopped turning, it stopped singing. The children all turned to stare at her, their breath obscuring their faces every other second.

Emma couldn't think of what to say, and then she sneezed, repeatedly again and again. The children all took a step backwards. Then they glanced at each other, and walked off wordlessly, splitting off in different directions. It was impossible for Emma to keep them all in view. The bell rang, muffled by the fog. She stood coughing and sniffing for a few seconds, wanting to call out to her class. But she couldn't speak and she watched their forms fade and become indistinguishable in the mist.

The rest of the day was without real occurrence. The class continued to seem wary and unresponsive, but she wasn't sure how much this was true and how much was just caused by her aching, fuzzy head.

The song the children had been singing seemed to stick with her and follow her home. She tried to ignore it when she got back to her flat, but the song seemed to hum in her head every time she coughed or sneezed or shivered uncontrollably. Unlike other memories, she couldn't banish this from her mind. She remembered the version *she'd* sung at school:

"Ring a ring a rosie,

"A pocketful of posies,

"Atishoo! Atishoo!

"We all fall down."

It seemed such a long time ago to her, but also still very clear, a perfect memory she hadn't examined in years. Emma was very good at locking things up inside of herself and pretending they'd never happened. But hearing the song again had made her feel very young, as if the years in-between had all just been a game, a dressing up game... She shook her head to rid herself of this ridiculous feeling, and moaned softly as the pain flared up again. The tablets she'd taken didn't seem to have had any noticeable effect.

Only twelve years, she thought, but so much has happened. Puberty, boys, men – who'd quickly become boys again. Big school, college, university, and then a job, a new city... And yet she could still remember, if she chose to, turning with the turning circle and singing the words that the circle sang...

She realised, without wanting to, that she must have been singing that song around the time her Aunt Jess had come to stay with them. After the doctor had said it was just a matter of time. Aunt Jess had had nowhere else to go, so she had come to stay with them, and Emma has been forced to kiss her goodnight; she'd kissed her on the forehead and each night it was as if the skin of it had pulled even tighter across her aunt's skull. Some nights, waking semi-conscious into the darkness of her bedroom, Emma had been convinced that a shrivelled version of Aunt Jess was lurking in the blackness, ready to reach out with her reed-thin arms to clasp Emma tight to her breast. She had realised on those nights not that her aunt was going to die, but that *she* was. And realising this she had shoved it down out of her mind's eye and successfully ignored it ever since – *she* wasn't going to die...

She couldn't remember her aunt's death, just her dying.

Emma went and poured herself a glass of wine, trying not to think back to that time. She thought instead of her children singing that song, and what she could teach them about it: the first line referred to the first visible signs of the plague, the blotchy red and black sores of the afflicted. The second was about the flowering herbs people had hoped would ward off the disease. Which didn't work of course, for then came the sneezing. And then they all fell down...

She sneezed herself, loud in the silent flat. Her nose felt raw as she blew it, and she couldn't stop shivering, as if she had caught a chill outside. She sat down and tried to distract herself with television, but all the programmes seemed too bright and loud.

Before heading to bed she took twice the recommended dose of some flu remedy. Alongside the wine this didn't so much help her sleep as knock her out – she felt just as ill the next day. But she was glad she had slept, and so quickly, for just before slipping away her mind had been full of the most sinister combination of fears, both grown up and childish.

Emma anxiously ran her hands up and down her throat – in the mirror it looked like someone small was strangling her. The swelling in her neck had definitely abated. But she still remembered Carl Burke's words ("the victim suffers fevers, swollen lymph glands..."), matter of fact and undramatic, as though describing his own reality. Emma shivered; her flat seemed cold despite the central heating.

When she left for work the world outside seemed as under the weather as she did, the air infected by murky fog, the day-old puddles rippled by an apathetic half-wind. Because she was so tired the mist seemed to follow Emma into the school, making everything seem fuzzy and ill-defined. In the staff room she heaped masses of coffee and sugar into a mug; the other teachers stared at her but didn't comment, at least until Emma left the room. She resisted the urge to crouch and listen at the keyhole; she told herself she didn't care what they thought of her. Unlike her class, suddenly so sullen and suspicious, the other teachers had *always* seemed to resent her somewhat. At least some things hadn't changed. But part of Emma still wanted to be included in their warmth and forty-something chatter.

When she entered the classroom the children were all sitting in their proper places, their hands crossed in their laps; she couldn't help but feel suspicious. Despite the rules no class ever waited completely still and silent. She knew she was being ridiculous and paranoid, yet the feeling remained. She greeted them, turned her back to wipe yesterday's lesson from the board

– someone whispered something but she couldn't catch the words.

All morning she couldn't shake the feeling that the children were *too* well behaved, and the smile on her face felt forced and sickly. Every time she had her back to them she was sure she heard voices whispering and giggling, but when she turned to see the children were just starring right back at her.

An hour before lunch she told them to get out their maths books; there were fewer petty insubordinations or requests for help than mathematics lessons normally provoked, and Emma took this as a bad sign. She walked up and down the rows of desks, as if stalking the whispering sound she could still hear, but her ears were ringing slightly and all her instincts seemed lost in the haze of her illness. And even though she knew the flu was going round every time one of the children coughed or sneezed she was irrationally sure it was faked and somehow mocking. But when she glared at them was their reaction innocence or just a good pretence?

She walked around the tables, observing each child's large, unsteady numbers adding up to the wrong answer; she was looking over Carl Burke's shoulder when behind her a girl screamed.

Emma turned round, so quickly that the room seemed to tilt around her. Lorraine Chambers had leapt from her chair, causing it to clatter over. The girl was cowering up against one wall, visibly shaking, on tip-toe as if to get as far away from the floor as possible. Her small hands were held up to her face, just beneath her eyes, which were starring at the floor.

"What is it? What's wrong, Lorraine?" Emma asked, her voice slightly more shaken than the situation demanded (Lorraine was one of her favourites). The girl looked at her with large, nakedly afraid eyes.

"A rat!" she said. "I saw *a rat* under the table!"

Emma felt her worst fears die – it was just something the girl had imagined. But the girl was obviously scared, she obviously *believed*, she'd seen a rat, so Emma walked towards her, mumbling maternally, and went to put her arm around the girl's shoulders. Lorraine shrank back from her, her eyes wide.

"Keep away from me!" she said. "Don't *touch* me!"

Emma recoiled from the seven year old's harsh and terrified words, not knowing what to think or do. She was aware of all the other children watching the two of them, not gaping as she would have expected, but with narrow lips and eyes and adult expressions. Emma's heart was pounding and for a dizzy second she had to steady herself against the wall. She couldn't let the situation slide out of her influence.

"Lorraine," she started, "Lorraine, listen to me. There wasn't a rat, you just imagined..."

"There was!"

"There wasn't," Emma said firmly. "Listen, no one else saw a rat did they?" She appealed to the class: "None of you saw a rat did you?" But none of them answered, they just sat and stared and smiled. Emma ignored the way they were smiling, she had too much to deal with already. She closed her eyes, and tried to gather strength behind them.

"You see Lorraine, sometimes our imaginations can play tricks on us. It's just like part of our dreams left over in daytime. But that doesn't make them real..."

After much persuasion Lorraine grew calmer and returned to her seat. She avoided the gaze of all the other children, who seemed angry with her, as if her behaviour reflected badly upon them all. They said nothing to her; Emma tried to imagine it was because they didn't know what to say. The whole incident had left her even more tired and drained than before, and her head and sinuses were throbbing abominably. She tried not to think about the way Lorraine had recoiled from her; it seemed too confusing to think about right now. She was relieved when the bell rang for lunch and the children filed out, talking amongst themselves. Lorraine Chambers trailed after them, alone, looking down at her dragging feet. The girl glanced at her briefly, and her eyes still seemed afraid. It seemed to Emma that she and Lorraine were in a way united, although she had no idea how or against what. But she liked the idea. Lorraine was one of her *favourites*.

"Miss Anderson? Are you... Miss Anderson?"

The voice roughly shook Emma awake, suddenly blinking bolt upright in her staff room chair. Slowly the shape of the face of one of the other teachers came into focus; Mrs Bennett had her hand on Emma's shoulder and she was still shaking her even though Emma was now obviously awake. Emma felt the dream she had been having fall away, for a few seconds its dark images lingered in her mind, before real life swung fully back into focus.

"You were asleep," Mrs Bennett said in the same voice she used to talk to the children.

"I... yes, I..."

"You may have been able to stay up all hours when you were a *student*," Mrs Bennett said, as if the word were distasteful and she had never been one, "but now you have to be responsible. You're lucky Mr Hall didn't catch you. You're lucky *I* won't tell him."

Emma bit back her instinctive response and instead muttered something humble. She felt the other teacher was crowding her, standing too close, and so she stood up, but too quickly and the blood seemed to drain from her head. Mrs Bennett still looked at her disapprovingly but turned ponderously around.

Acting on instinct, Emma called her back.

"I just wondered," she said quickly, "the substitute teacher who took my class while I was sick? What... what was he like?"

When she turned back around Mrs Bennett's eyes were the only hard points in her flabby face. But they gradually defused and looked further away; her pinched mouth parted slightly.

"He was..." She paused, changed tack. "I'm sure they wouldn't send anyone *inappropriate*. But..."

"But?" prompted Emma. A boy ran past the staff room window, screaming and laughing – "*Keep away!*" Mrs Bennett appeared not to notice.

"He was odd. Always dark clothes but very pale skin. I mean it is March but... Very slim, too slim surely? To be healthy..."

"*Urgghhh! Keep away!*" the boy outside screamed.

"He seemed to think he was better than everyone else," Mrs Bennett continued tartly. "And spoke to us in put on voices...."

"Urggghhhh! You've got the lurgee!"

Mrs Bennett shuddered slightly (Emma wasn't sure the other woman realised she was doing so) and returned to the present. Her eyes hardened again as they saw Emma.

"Why?" she said loudly, fat wobbling. "Is there a problem?" Her tone suggested it would be Emma's fault if there was.

"Oh, no problem," Emma said. And there wasn't, was there? She sneezed suddenly and with no warning, and Mrs Bennett shuddered and walked away without a word. Emma sneezed a few more times ("Atishoo! Atishoo!" her mind chanted) and then sighed as she realised she'd slept through her break and didn't have time to eat. She just took two painkillers, washing them down with cold coffee from the mug by her chair, where she had dreamt and then forgotten

Emma shouldn't have been on playground duty that afternoon but another teacher was off sick ("It's this damn flu going around," Mr Hall said, looking at Emma) so she'd volunteered. She had no desire to sit with the rest of the teachers anyway. Nevertheless she wondered if it had been a mistake as she stood in the cold and tried not to shiver. Maybe she was too sick to have come back to work so soon...

She looked around the concrete sweep of the playground, at the pale and poorly looking sun already sinking. She looked to see if her class were again playing on their own, singing that old song under the shadow of the climbing frame. But she was relieved to see they weren't; her class must be playing with the other children again, mixed up in all the running and screaming...

She stared and stared, trying to peer through the mist and sleep-lack smudges that stained her vision – she couldn't see *any* of the children from her class at all. Where were they all? She tried to think but everything conspired to make it difficult – she turned round slowly, as if the air were clinging, and when she started to run towards the school the bell rang and a hundred, a thousand, children rushed past her, as if she were moving in slow motion; a school of children tight together as fish, knocking her aside – but not hers, not Lorraine or any of the others.

She burst into Mr Hall's office without knocking; he was on the phone and gestured angrily for her to leave but she refused.

"My class have disappeared!"

Mr Hall looked at her, his eyes dangerously bright.

"Ah, you'll have to excuse me," he said calmly into the receiver. "One of the children is playing up. Yes. Yes, goodbye." He put the phone down, then said, "Please explain yourself, Miss Anderson."

"In the playground... *none* of my children were there!" Emma said.

"I'm sure you're mistaken about that," Mr Hall said.

"We have to call..."

"We have to do no such thing. I'm sure your children were there, you just didn't see them among all the others, what with the fog and your, ah, tiredness. After all you were sick for such a long time you must be tired. I'm sure your class is sitting in their classroom, waiting for their teacher."

"But they weren't..."

"Let's just check the classroom before doing anything rash, shall we?"

They walked towards her classroom, and when they got there she saw all her children sitting there, starring.

"There you are, Miss Anderson," Mr Hall said, enjoying himself. "All present and correct."

But Emma wasn't listening for she was starring at Lorraine Chambers, who was trying to avoid her gaze. But the girl had obviously been crying – was she *still* doing so? Emma saw the girl's body shake. She went towards her, making soothing noises, careful not to touch her for she remembered how the girl had reacted previously. Lorraine just stared with miserable intensity at the desk in front of her.

She glared around the class. "Have any of you been bullying Lorraine? Picking on her?"

The class shook its head. "No, Miss Anderson," it chorused.

"Where were you all during playtime?"

Mr Hall snorted, and left. Emma ignored him for her question seemed to have caught the children off guard; they glanced at each other before answering. Emma felt her paranoia deepening, and tried to struggle above it. Eventually a few kids answered reluctantly:

"The playground."

"No you weren't," Emma said "I was on playground duty this afternoon and I didn't see any of you."

There was a pause, then Michael Potts said,

"You weren't supposed to be on playground duty today, Miss," and she realised they had planned to do something, something somewhere, when they thought she wouldn't realise.

But what? They were seven year olds – surely her thoughts were ridiculous?

Emma decided they were, they must be. She shook her head, the outward reflection of her inner denial. She told the children to get out their spelling books, and she ignored (with a pang) the still snivelling Lorraine. Her head started to ache painfully again, setting the tone for what remained of the day.

She couldn't sleep that night, her fever a suffocating thing keeping her awake in the darkness. She alternately kicked the duvet off because she felt hot and stifled, and drew it up to her neck shivering. There was a streetlight outside Emma's room which was faulty, and its flickering light kept making the shadows change shape around her. The people in the flat above were having noisier sex than her parents had ever had, panting and screaming like it was their last night alive.

Emma turned, trying to get comfortable, trying to block out the noises from above. The light outside flickered and her eyes opened, and the shadows were like stick-thin arms reaching for her...

The Black Death killed one in five Europeans she thought – she had looked it up that evening on the internet. She wasn't quite sure why she had, but thoughts about her children, about Lorraine, had tormented her and it had at least felt like she was doing something. One in five – that was about the same as cancer she supposed. She tried not to think that we had just exchanged one plague for others, ones that left us a little longer, but it was hard to push such thoughts aside in the darkness. She didn't want to think of her own mortality; how could *she* die? Emotionally it held no truth for her – surely a cure-all would be found, the rules changed before death claimed her...

Aunt Jess, she thought, and then sneezed herself fully awake. She remembered how she had used to be scared that her dying aunt had been hiding in wardrobe, on sleepless nights very much like this one. She opened her eyes – because of the shadows it was impossible to tell if her wardrobe was open or not. It never shut properly anyway, so it wouldn't signify anything if it was open. Wouldn't mean it had been *pushed* open – you're not a child anymore, Emma told herself angrily, and turned over and curled up before finally willing herself asleep.

The next morning, during break time, Emma went out into the playground again, not offering the other teachers a word of explanation. The fog was if anything thicker, semi-solid and twisting. The school children's enthusiasm was undampened however; they played their games just as noisily and chaotically, as if the mist were only in Emma's eyes. But she had no problem spotting her class, clumped together and sneaking off round a corner of the school building, thinking they weren't being watched. The corner led to the back of the school kitchens, where the large dustbins stood. The children would be undisturbed there to... what? Emma tried to think, but her thoughts seemed lost in the fog and impossible to focus on... and she wasn't sure she wanted to see anyway. She decided she wouldn't go and confront the children yet. She would wait and try and speak to Lorraine alone (Lorraine was her favourite). And who knew – maybe there was a perfectly natural explanation and Emma's fears were groundless.

She was sitting at her desk waiting for her class when they filed back in, and she tried to give them the same all-knowing look that Mr Hall or Mrs Bennett could manage so effortlessly. But the children just glanced at her and smiled; could they see the uncertainty in her eyes? In any case the effect was ruined when Emma started to cough and sneeze; tears filled her eyes and the children all merged in her eyes as she blinked them back. The class seemed to smile to itself as she stood up to teach, as if they were the adults and she the child, and they were just tolerating her infantile games.

They were still smiling in the same way when Emma noticed that there was an empty seat in the classroom. Lorraine had not returned from break time.

Emma felt nauseous; her throat felt dry and tasted of phlegm.

"Where's Lorraine?" she managed to say.

No response save for twenty-six smiles.

"Where's *Lorraine?*" she repeated. "I know you were all playing with her at break."

"She wasn't with us, Miss Anderson," Jo Webster said. Emma turned and banged her hands on the desk in front of the girl, causing her momentarily to flinch.

"I *saw* her go with you!"

Jo glanced at her classmates before replying. Her words seemed tightly controlled.

"She wasn't with us, Miss."

Emma stared at her class, but couldn't meet the gaze of any of them for more than a few seconds. She felt a sick feeling in her stomach and head that was more than just the lingering effects of her illness.

"Stay here all of you," she said, and headed towards the classroom door.

"She was chosen. She was *it*," a voice said behind her.

She wasn't sure who had spoken or which direction the voice had come from, and when she turned all of the class wore identical expressions of innocence.

"Who said that?" she said. There was silence. "*Who said that?*" she said, her face flaming. She wasn't used to such anger and she felt her hands trembling slightly as she walked slowly back towards the children. She wasn't sure what the expression on her face was like, but finally they looked like they were frightened of her...

"Just what is going on in here?" Mr Hall said from the doorway, smirking.

Lorraine's family couldn't be contacted, but Mr Hall didn't seem concerned. He had the caretaker search the school grounds but refused to phone the police until he'd spoken to her parents. He assured Emma that the girl would turn up soon, and treated the whole thing like an annoyance that was somehow her fault.

"What about the substitute teacher who took my class?" Emma said. "He might know something; shouldn't we call him?"

"Mr Markham?" Mr Hall said, frowning. "What on earth would he know? He was just a substitute teacher, despite what he might have thought."

"What do you mean by that?"

"He won't be coming here again, sickness or no sickness, put it that way. I'd rather teach the children myself." The headmaster seemed to shudder slightly as he spoke.

"But what...?" Emma started.

"Miss Anderson, he was a bad teacher, that's all. We do get them you know." He stared at her meaningfully. "If you must know he worked to undermine me. Harried some of the other teachers..."

"Harried how..?"

"*And* he wasted my time," Mister Hall said. "Much as you are now. It is lunch time you know." He got up and left Emma alone in his own office, ignoring her continued questions.

She wasn't hungry, and during the lunch break when she knew all the children and teachers were in the dining room, Emma went to the place where she guessed her class had been sneaking off to at playtimes. It was a small quadrangle round the back of the kitchens, blocked off from sunlight on three sides by the school buildings, and it was full of tall bins. The shadows were so thick as to be like fog, even in the daytime, and the tight box-like dimensions of the place made Emma feel claustrophobic. The bins were higher than she was, and stank of decay. Black flies buzzed and jostled; some had fallen and lay on their backs, spinning occasionally with high cries, their legs feeble. Something larger had seemed to move behind one of the bins, and Emma's first thought was that it was a rat, until she told herself that was ridiculous.

She didn't know what she was looking for – she certainly didn't expect to find Lorraine – and she actually found nothing at all. But she knew with an unshakable belief that her class of children had been here. There was room for all of them certainly, between the stinking bins.

There was even room for them to stand in a circle, if they wished.

He called her late at night after she'd drunk a whole bottle of wine on top of the medicine she was taking, and the whole thing seemed unreal the next morning, like a drunken memory so unlikely it didn't form a link with events before or after. Nonetheless she was convinced it was real, that it had happened.

"How did you get my number?" was the first thing she said after he introduced himself, but Mr Markham just laughed.

"Don't you want to talk to me? Aren't there things you want to ask?"

"Wh... what?" she said groggily.

"Then let me help you. Have the disappearances started yet?"

Emma felt her head pound; felt like the background static hum of the phone was in her own ears. Everything seemed dulled and fuzzy like her flu was sheltering her from the world.

"Let me see," he said, "who would it be first I wonder... Michael Potts? Lorraine Chambers?"

"How..?" Emma said. "Has Mister Hall...?"

Markham's laughter cut her off; he seemed to be enjoying himself.

"No, no," he said, sounding like an mocking actor who didn't believe in his part. "I just suspected it would be her. She wasn't as... receptive, shall we say, as some of the others. Already so grown up for her age! So I figured her for the first scapegoat."

"Scapegoat?"

"Maybe sacrifice is a better word," Markham said, as if good-naturedly conceding a point. "To appease a few gods perhaps. You won't find her body you know."

Emma closed her eyes and entered the darkness where her headache boomed. Eyes shut none of it seemed real, not possibly real at all, and she jumped when Markham spoke in the darkness.

"There's nothing to find. Which is the only truth, or suggestive of it anyway. Just like all that medieval shite I taught them. And just like your Aunt Jess, cancer-thin and coming for you. For *you*."

"How did you *know...?*"

Markham laughed. When he spoke next Emma was vaguely aware his voice had changed, as if he'd changed parts. He sounded like some fusty academic.

"Of course your 'monster', your 'Aunt Jess' was a very pure example of the archetype, undiluted one might say. Because all of childhood's monsters represent one thing in the end..."

"Where's Lorraine?" Emma interrupted, her head pounding, but Markham barely paused. Instead his voice changed again, became frantic, almost aggressive:

"... one thing only! And contrary to what you think now, all grown up and repressed Emma, it will get you, one day, the monster will *get* you and take you with it..."

"Be quiet!" Emma said, but her blocked nose made her anger sound feeble. She couldn't think with this madman's voice infecting her thought processes. Before she could gather her wits he was off again, with yet another voice. He didn't just sound child-like, he sounded exactly like a child: high-pitched, mocking, malevolent:

"Ring around the rosie,

"A pocketful of posies,

"Ashes, atisho!

"Who falls down?"

Emma's head span with the words; surely this man, who sounded insane, couldn't be a teacher? But then as soon as she thought that his voice became adult again, stern, authoritative – exactly like a teacher's.

"Of course you know what the posy was for?" he said. Emma answered automatically.

"To... they thought it would protect them..."

"Gold star Emma! Many prayed too of course, thinking God would protect *them*, if no one else. But He didn't. But people still wanted protection, from anyone, anything. And some people remembered old songs, old even then... "

Emma sneezed thunderously, unexpectedly, and this seemed to interrupt the voice where her stammered words couldn't, to throw him off his stride.

"I don't care about any of that!" she said quickly whilst he was silent. "I don't care about *history*, I care about what's happening now. Where's Lorraine?"

But he had recovered, and his voice had changed again.

"Don't you think, Emma, that in her last instant your Aunt Jess would have sacrificed anyone – absolutely anyone, including you – to save herself?"

Then there was blankness and then it was as if she had awoken some time after the conversation had ended, although that couldn't be the case. Emma still had the phone pressed to her ear and her eyes closed. She swayed slightly with the wine and affects of her tablets, and she wasn't sure which of them it was who had hung up or when.

Lorraine didn't turn up; Emma spoke to the girl's mother on the phone the next day, and the franticness in the other woman's voice made Emma feel sick. She didn't mention the conversation she'd had with Markham; the fact that he'd said the body wouldn't be found. She hadn't told anyone she'd spoken to Markham, not having anyone to tell, and not quite believing it had happened. When she put the phone down she looked out of the office windows – the fog seemed to be thinning, but revealing black clouds crowding the sky and beating it downwards.

Mr Hall had been listening to Emma's call the whole time (he had refused to speak to the parents himself, although he'd have to speak to the police later) and now he impatiently gestured for her to leave his office. He didn't seem to feel the deep lurking panic that Emma did. She went back to her classroom, and her children barely seemed to be hiding their whispered conversations now, their looks of smiling contempt at what she had to teach them. And it did seem to Emma something paltry; sums and spellings thrown in the face of death.

She couldn't stop thinking that, despite being young, she knew a lot of people who had died. Not just her Aunt Jess, but also a girl from school (in a car crash at seventeen), three grandparents (two strokes, one cancer); a little boy before that, bald and with a tube in his nose at age seven which none of the kids had understood, and then he'd been gone from class one day. And a man at a factory where she had worked one summer, who had got pulled somehow into the roaring machinery while Emma's back had been turned (and as the screaming panic had started behind her she'd kept her back turned, thinking that if she didn't look then it couldn't affect her). She couldn't stop thinking about all these deaths, which perhaps made up for the small amount she had thought about them before. But it still didn't all seem quite real to her. Death was something that happened to other people. She didn't believe in it, not in any way that seriously threatened her...

But Lorraine. She could, just, imagine Lorraine being dead if she set her mind to it. Or rather, if her mind set itself to it, for she seemed to have little control over the images it projected into the spaces behind her eyes. Lorraine had always been one of her favourites and she had failed to protect her...

The bell rang for the afternoon break, the final one of the week. The children got up, their eyes directly challenging hers. They seemed more sombre now, but still beyond her, out of her influence. There was a forced swagger in their gaits, like teenagers walking past a group of the opposite sex. They walked like this past Emma now; something in their manner convinced her that this was *it*, somehow, the last chance to alter anything or find out what was going on with them.

Emma got up and followed directly behind them, like she was a child too.

This seemed to surprise them but not concern them unduly. The children walked in a row outside – the fog was thinning visibly now, black shapes and shadows emerging from its tight grey sheeting. The tension of an impending storm fell from the massed clouds above, proceeding the raindrops themselves. The change in pressure seemed to clear Emma's head, for her thoughts seemed faster and freer than they had all week, although she still felt a clot of wordless fear in the centre that she couldn't articulate much less relieve.

The children ignored her, and proceeded round the side of the playground, to the quadrangle. No one talked.. Emma, at the back of the line, didn't know how to assert her authority. She stood aimlessly beside one of the overflowing bins, the smell adding to her nausea. The secret quadrangle was darker and colder than everywhere else, washed over by shadows. The light seemed to be visibly fading as the children, watched helplessly by Emma, held hands and formed a circle. She expected them to start singing, the song Markham had no doubt taught them ("we all fall down") – instead Michael Potts raised his left hand and pointed at the girl next to him. Without meeting anyone's eyes he chanted a childish rhyme, which trembled with his voice:

"Ip, dip, dog, shit, you, trod, in, it, and, O, U, T, spells, out."

With each syllable he moved his pointing finger one along the circle of children; the girl branded "out" breathed a visible sigh of relief. The dipping continued, this time with another rhyme:

"Ip, dip, sky, blue, it, is, not, you, and, O, U, T, spells, out."

Alternating between these two rhymes more and more children became "out" and all looked relieved. But the tension, rather than lessening, increased; Emma could feel it spitting between the children like it was spitting between the storm clouds above, which were creating a wall of darkness atop shadowy walls.

Only Michael Potts and Rebecca Beckett were left in. Michael diligently started the rhyme, but all the children, and Emma, worked out before he'd finished that he'd be out and Rebecca left in.

The two children on either side of Rebecca left go of her hands; she turned in mute appeal to them, her mouth working at the air. The other children pushed her into the centre and joined hands again, the circle becoming one link smaller around her. Rebecca turned slowly looking at her classmates, silent but her eyes pleading. Emma realised the girl looked absolutely terrified. The other children looked at their feet and started to turn...

"No!" shouted Emma, reminding them of her presence. Markham's words seemed to be running through her thoughts: "scapegoat", "sacrifice", "ashes, ashes". She had no idea what was happening, but saw Rebecca's eyes look to her like she was her last hope. Emma rushed forward and pushed into the centre of the circle. The children didn't say anything. Emma took Rebecca's hand and started to led her out of the quadrangle...but when the girl got to the edge of the circle she simply turned round, took the two proffered hands, and returned to her previous place. Her eyes looked anywhere but at Emma.

The circle started to turn again, with Emma in its eye. The children started to sing:

"Ring around the rosie,

"A pocketful of posies..."

Their voices didn't sound innocent, but fully aware of the song's history and connotations.

Emma stood there, watching the children turn, not knowing what to do. Each time the song was repeated it was faster, and the circle turned faster. The children's faces turned passt her, blurred into generalities. Because of the shadows and clouds she felt like she was in a tight black box, full of the smell of rot and decay. She remembered singing this song, and it seemed to her that the faces of some of those she had sang it with were amongst those which turned and turned around her. She felt dizzy and unstable, like she could fall down just because the song lyrics suggested it. The circle whirled faster, sang faster, and Emma closed her eyes.

In the darkness she saw Aunt Jess, shrunken and deathbound and reaching out for her, to embrace her... but that embrace would pull her into the darkness too, Emma saw. She saw herself reflected in her aunt's pupils, a tiny child Emma caught in the darkness and screaming, realising what every child realises and immediately represses.

The circle was singing different words now, older ones perhaps, which Emma heard in her darkness – they were unintelligible but expressive, and they were sung with childish total belief. There wasn't any monster in her wardrobe really, only blackness... not even her Aunt Jess just blackness, which was worse, much worse. It was nothing and too much. As the song was sung knowledge awoke and arose in her, spreading outwards and infecting everything, turning the spinning centre of every atom black. She was no longer sure if her eyes were open or not and it no longer mattered, because everything was black. Everything was black and everything was consumed, and she knew she was consumed too. She was consumed and she was going to die; she believed it finally and totally because the song and the circle made her believe it. And believing it and absorbing it would make it so; she felt herself falling down, falling away into the blackness, and she knew, with the total fascination that the dying reserve for their final thought, that the others around her were glad that at least, this time, it hadn't been *them*.

And then the circle stopped turning, and Emma fell down.

DRONES

The rest of the soldiers call me 'Drone' because that's what I fly – UAVs. Unmanned drones that can circle battlefields many kilometres wide, and deliver a precise Hellfire strike against any target in that zone, all based on commands from my computer terminal back at base. That distance in part accounts for my contemptuous nickname, of course – the pilots, the artillery, the medics, the infantry (especially the fucking infantry) are all in the firing line at some point, all in some theoretical danger even from the ragtag bunch of guerrillas we are fighting in the mountains. Whereas I am watching events on a screen miles behind the rest of them. They treat me like one of the civilian bureaucrats, and not like someone who has trained and fought alongside them, someone who has saved their ass on occasion.

There are other UAV pilots than me of course, but only I am 'Drone' and I know they mean something disparaging about my manner by this as well. I am not *against* this war (how could I be, when back home so many people voted for and continue to vote for the politicians who launched it?) but I feel no jingoistic bloodlust or hatred for our enemy either. Flying drones is what I have been trained to do, so I do it, in a manner I like to think is both precise and competent.

The enemy would be hard to hate anyway, for I barely see them. The screen I stare at is usually the washed out and ghostly green of night-vision, and I see the compound, the truck convoy, the tanks, but rarely the people. Even if I do they are just glowing smudges of infrared heat. I know the missile is on its way before they do – the numbers count down in the bottom-right of the screen. When they reach zero my screen fills with pixelated white light, and then the image returns, but emptier.

The drones can only send back visuals not sound of course, so the strikes seem to take place in complete silence. If anything it seems even *more* silent afterwards, unless someone squawks their aggressive congratulations into my ear-pierce. But I am already back, flying the drone to wherever the plan says it needs to be next.

Back home, when driving I'll sometimes arrive somewhere and not remember the drive there – I've negotiated traffic, manoeuvred round junctions, and even changed the radio station, all without conscious thought. Just conditioned reactions to the world on the other side of my windscreen.

This job is like that – trained reaction to stimulus. If I've fired I can normally remember the screen pooling with light, but not the decision-points, not the reasoning that got me, and them, to that destination.

Today was a fuck up and people are angry. 'Friendly fire' – I agree with them it's a slimy, mealy-mouthed phrase. We are supposed to be fighting for these people, whether they want us here or not, and that means alongside their 'official' army (some of whom are as young as sixteen but everyone turns a blind eye) but instead there was a fuck up and somehow a convoy of their jeeps and artillery returning *back* from enemy territory was identified as coming directly *from* enemy territory. Attack helicopters were dispatched, but my drone was already in the air.

I was hardly at fault so I don't see why everyone is looking at me like they are. I didn't identify them as the enemy, someone else did, and once that identification was made everything was just a matter of protocols, and training, and numbers counting down... The numbers had already started falling when my earpiece squealed there was an error – I can deliver strikes from miles away but obviously once I've fired they can't be recalled. They tried to radio them, but *another* fuck up means their troops and ours use incompatible equipment most of the time...

I didn't look away, I watched the screen until it went white. Maybe the signal had interference (or maybe it was just sand in the computer again) but the white wasn't total this time, it had faint structure. Almost like...

But that must have been something I added to the memory afterwards, from guilt.

I do feel guilt, despite what the others think of me. But feeling guilty doesn't make me to *blame*.

I am off active duty until it has been looked into.

It will be hushed up of course, the media don't really care unless some of our troops are killed. And who would they be to start accusing people anyway? All the newspapers and TV stations supported the war, just like all the politicians who voted for it, and everyone who voted for *them*. If people make a decision they can't blame the people who carry out that decision if it's the wrong one. And everyone knows war is messy and chaotic – despite all the rules how could it not be, with all this pent up emotion always behind its logic? Not my emotions you understand, but I can feel it in others: in the way they shout over the mic, in the kill-tallies they paint on the sides of choppers and tanks, in the way they stomp sand from their boots and glare at me.

As predicted, I am back on active duty. I have been cleared of all blame – it is true that if I had been slower the order to abort the attack would have come in time, but they can hardly blame me for being *competent*. A few here at the base still give me funny looks but mostly they understand.

I actually feel a little nervous about tonight's mission; it's like being home from duty and driving for the first time in months, and it feels odd and unnatural for a few minutes, until you reacclimatise. Briefly, the stresses and dangers of driving seem real again. I feel like that about tonight's mission, although I will be fine once it has begun. Maybe it is a lingering reaction to how that silent white light looked when we knew we'd targeted the wrong side; how it had briefly looked like a face.

It happened again.

We'd been given orders to strike the industrial quarter of a small town in the lowlands – Intel said it had been cleared out of workers and was being used as a military supply point and refuelling station.

I knew from the scale and scope of the operation that I'd get a chance to fire. Maybe a few times (my UAV carries up to six Hellfire missiles). I was nervous to start with, as expected, but then my training took over and I can't recall much until I was watching the numbers count down as the missile neared its target. I was calm then, so nerves can't have explained what happened. Sometimes you just know it will be a clean and precise strike, and I knew that this time.

My screen flared white and I was already starting to think about the next target when a dark, pixelated face flared out of that whiteness, and then another and another, and I knew they were all the men I had just killed. They looked out of the screen at me with hatred.

I didn't mean to but I cried out into my microphone. Of course I recovered myself, didn't tell anyone what I had seen.

When I had to fire again I looked away from the screen at the crucial moment, so that it wouldn't happen again. That *hatred*...

Rumour has of course got out that 'Drone' shrieked across the airwaves, that 'Drone' sounded like he was afraid even though he (and only he) was in no danger. People are looking at me oddly again. I feel that nausea I get when confronted by problems I can't solve by reason alone.

I mustn't let it happen again.

I can't keep doing this, I can't keep looking away or closing my eyes every time I fire. Even behind closed lids the flash of light is white enough to penetrate, so that I almost see the faces each time even then. Seem to feel their hatred straining to reach me. And their disdain, for the enemy, these soldiers, are just like those on my side – they despise me for killing them from a position where I can't be killed myself; from the other side of a computer screen.

A few times I have tried to stare them out – to look into their faces in the bright light of the fire I have delivered and meet their gaze: men, boys, and women (we know we sometimes target civilians by mistake, but another blind eye is turned). To prove to them that it is not *my* fault; that the decisions, the votes, were not mine. But their hatred and disdain always makes me look away first.

I am to be transferred back home due to 'stress'. They want me to quit of course – far easier for them if I just leave rather than have to try and discharge me due to a psychological condition that started whilst on active duty. Ungrateful bastards. But I will oblige.

"Bye Drone; see you Drone" – I am glad to get away.

~

It's three months since I was discharged; I am shivering in a cold house because I can't afford to pay the bills. (It feels so fucking cold here after being *there*.) I can't get a job that I can hold down because I can't work anywhere with *screens*.

It started on the flight back; it was a civilian flight and in each seat people had screens folded down from the roof to watch the in-flight movie. I didn't pull down mine, but I could still see everyone else's out of the corner of my eye... especially when they seemed to slow, and show numbers counting down in the bottom-right, and then flash with bright light and hatred that washed over me in my seat. I sat clenched and terrified staring out the window; I was sick but not for the reason the air hostess thought.

It has been happening more and more since I got back; and there are so many screens everywhere nowadays! My house is full of them – my TV, my laptop, my mobile – I have had to turn them all off. The GPS in my car blinding me; the screens in shopping centres showing adverts until *I* pass, when they fill with silent faces. TV shops with each screen in the window a single, separate face. (Have I killed so many?) And of course, any office I try and get a temp job in is open plan and full of PCs. I try to focus on the meaningless document or spreadsheet of numbers I am working on, when suddenly the numbers began falling and I knew what will happen when the countdown reaches zero...

Closing my eyes doesn't help; crying out doesn't help although I do it anyway and the whole office turns to stare. Before I am asked to leave I have no doubt acquired a nickname or two; I am still 'Drone' despite leaving the war.

I don't know how to stop seeing the faces – my parents wanted to show me a photo on their digital camera of their first grandchild (my brother's daughter) and how could I have said no? But then I flinched and dropped their camera (it didn't smash) when the screen filled with light only I could see, and a face that promised me damnation in return for that I had visited on her.

But why me? There's a whole army and air-force killing them all the time, and everyone I pass on the street lets it *happen*, so why me?

It may be over. For some reason I was feeling defiant today, and I plugged in my TV for the first time in months. By coincidence I watched the news, showing troop movements and drone strikes after the event. For a brief moment I felt the old camaraderie and wished I was back there, despite all that has happened. And then, as I expected, the TV screen flooded with white, silent light...

I picked it up and smashed it against the floor just as the first face started to appear.

For a moment I thought, *You fool, you've let them out!* because I felt the light and the hatred surround me. I closed my eyes. I imagined their forms as I had seen them in my night-vision: amorphous and glowing ghosts. And I swear I felt something almost like a hand start to pull at me, to pull me down.

Then there was a pause, like consideration, and then nothing.

I opened my eyes – the TV was smoking with its screen cracked down the middle, and I was alone. After a few moments I cautiously turned on my mobile phone, which I've also not used for months. Its screen filled with the bright light of its maker's logo, but nothing more. It's been switched on for over an hour now, and nothing has happened. I will call my parents on it to apologise; hell, I may even *video* call them.

I think it will all be alright now.

It didn't make sense for a while, but now it does. I always knew I wasn't to blame, not solely at any rate. The people who voted for war or who just let it happen or profited from it – they are as guilty. Everyone I killed, I killed with thousands at my back.

It started with army personnel on leave – killed, seemingly torn apart in a frenzy when they were alone. No one understood how or why – the savagery, the speed. Like they'd been blown apart but without any explosion.

Then a politician was killed in the same way, and then a newspaper editor, and then the CEO of a munitions company. It was all the news talked about, and there was speculation that it was a new terrorist weapon, and that we should step up our war effort accordingly.

And then a petrol station attendant, ripped apart in his booth between customers, and that confused everyone because why would terrorists attack someone like that?

And then the people who were killed were just people, normal people – a few every day, but *more* every day too, seemingly at random across the country. All killed in the same hideous way. Everyone is terrified but no one knows why it is happening but me.

I *did* let them out, after all. And they understood where the blame lies, understood which army of people their hatred should be targeted against. I wonder who, if anyone, they will spare as guiltless? It is one thing to imagine their glowing, infrared forms descending on an adult; but on a child, a baby... I think they will care about such things as much as *we* did, out in the desert.

They still hate and despise me *more* than everyone else though – for being cowardly, in their eyes; from watching their deaths on a computer screen miles away from even the faintest chance of retaliation... That for them is the final insult and indignity.

They do hate me, so they are leaving *me* until last.

To watch, like I've always done.

PUBLIC INTEREST STORY

Outside, next morning, was a crowd.

Joel stood and watched them from the front bedroom, which afforded the best view. It was a *small* crowd, true, maybe a dozen people. But it was a crowd nonetheless – he could see that by the way they stood, not moving and close together, little bits of their personality rubbing off on each other. Their eyes glazed over with each other's mentality. The quick twitch of his curtains set them murmuring, started a couple of them pacing around. Someone shouted something, seemingly for the sake of it, but Joel couldn't make out the words. He let go of the curtain and sat down with his back to the wall, head below the window-line, arms around his knees. He looked at the dusty wooden floor of the bedroom, the bed stripped of bedclothes, the bare coat-hangers in the open wardrobe. There were still magazines and one shoe under the bed, which he hadn't noticed before. Ian had packed so quickly that he had left some stuff behind, but Joel didn't think his housemate would be coming back to get it. Joel licked his lip, where it had been cut. He heard another yell from outside.

That newspaper, he thought, this is all the fault of that fucking newspaper.

The two housemates had a newspaper each delivered every Sunday. Typically Joel and Ian would be sitting together, nursing hangover coffee, when the clattering, metallic sound battered at the doorway (the newspaper girl or boy was just a smudged shape behind frosted glass). Maybe it was the caffeine – maybe it was the hangover – but the sound of the paper being delivered always set Joel's nerves on edge.

It was always the smaller, tabloid-sized paper – Ian's paper – that was delivered first, with a brief clattering fanfare. Like something alive forcing its way in. Then Joel's paper struggled through, a more difficult and segregated birth. The broadsheet wouldn't fit through in one go and some of the sections – maybe Culture, maybe Escape – were pushed through separately. Even so, the main paper tended to rip, so that words of stories on page 3 and even 5 could be seen on page 1, hints of editorial decisions in an alternative universe.

Ian and Joel were not students, but still lived like they were. Joel didn't really know how he had ended up living with Ian – he had lost touch with other friends with whom he had been far closer. Although they got on, it was because Joel never argued with Ian's opinions, which he felt were frequently loud-mouthed and ill-informed. But then maybe Ian's gypsy-bashing and homophobia were really Devil's advocacy – Joel didn't actually know him well enough to be sure. So he said nothing and stayed living with Ian. Besides, the house was near to the dead-end street where he worked, and the rent was cheap for a double room (for what good the double did him).

Ian would always get up with a groan to go and fetch the papers, leaving Joel a few moments hanging suspended, reflecting. He would never quite admit to himself that this reflection made him even more anxious; nervous even – although he had been drifting since university, he still felt he must have made some drastic and ill-founded detour to have ended up living how he was. Somehow, when he looked at his life, it didn't seem quite *his*.

Ian would return with the papers, flinging the ungainly broadsheet at Joel in two parts. The headlines – the international tension, crisis recoveries, and exit plans – soothed him, gave his previous thoughts some perspective. The two lads would sit and read their papers, drinking their cooling coffee. Generally, Ian took as long to read his paper as Joel did his.

"I don't know why you read that shit," Joel would say at some point. When Ian finished with the tabloid Joel would pick it up between thumb and forefinger, like it was trash discarded. But still, he would always read it. It always seemed the same, and yet in the same heartbeat surreal, some dispatch from a country with which he had lost touch years ago. There were stories about celebrities he'd never heard of, agony-aunt columns whose advice seemed suicidal, constant froth about a soap opera royal family, editorials denouncing "mass immigration" from countries too small to be found on the map, tirades against "perverts and paedophiles" opposite the tits of an eighteen year old girl with a made up name. He felt strange reading it, like there was more meaning in the fuzzy print than he could decipher, like it was all set in a code that he should have learnt.

"Why do you always *read* it then, if it's so shit?" Ian would say.

Joel couldn't answer. Partly of course it was just sick fascination. He didn't find the views expressed repellent so much as ludicrous – an elaborate mythology scratched and re-scratched below the tide-line. So partly he read the paper on the know-your-enemy principle. But partly... he was also *looking* for something. For what exactly he didn't know – and indeed he was only half-conscious of the fact that he was looking for anything at all. But as he strived to make sense of the tabloid mindset, underneath there was the feeling that one day he would see *something* in there with a direct and vital relevance to his life.

BAN THIS FILTH! he read. HOW CAN THIS MONSTER BE ALLOWED OUT AMOUNG OUR KIDS? LEFTY LUNACY. 34DD.

"It's just trash," he would say to Ian, flinging it back with a faint but tangible feeling of disappointment. Of relief.

"Go back to your liberal crap," Ian would say. "There's enough of it."

There were more of them now – Joel watched from the bedroom as the newcomers were welcomed, absorbed into the crowd. They had come as a couple but they weren't looking at each other now, but upwards at his house like everyone else. Their expressions slackened to match those around them. The crowd all swayed with the same internal rhythm; all of their eyes remained fixed on the still point of the window. Why are you here? Joel thought. This is ridiculous! There was some shouting, which died down. He couldn't hear what they were shouting. The crowd moved – from above he could see the movement like ripples on flat water. He realised one person was pushing forwards, but he could barely see the man, just the wake either side of him as he moved people aside. When he reached the front of the crowd the man continued to run forward, a dark silhouette cutting across the lawn towards the front door. Joel heard the letterbox open and close, then the man ran back to where he had come from, creating new ripples in the crowd before those caused by his brief exit had even died away. Joel blinked in astonishment, and lost sight of the man. Then he ran downstairs, to the hall. When he saw what had been pushed through the letterbox it made some sense – maybe it would *all* start to make sense now.

Through the door had been pushed a rolled up tube of newspaper. Tabloid, Joel saw – it must be today's edition, and it would carry some *explanation*. But halfway to it, Joel's eager strides slowed; he could smell something. Kneeling to retrieve the paper it was unmistakable – shit. As he lifted the paper it sagged with weight, but didn't break; Joel gagged at the smell. The bastards have put shit through my door! he thought, not so much angry as simply incredulous. What had driven them to such a thing?

The dustbins were in the back garden, which was fortunately self-contained, so he could enter it without the people at the front of his house realising. Joel gripped the newspaper between thumb and forefinger, head averted, and flung it into the bin. He could hear the sound of the crowd from round front; a chant almost started up but the rhythm was lost this time, defused. Why? Joel thought again. Looking in the bin he could see the crap stained stories, the crumpling of the newspaper putting the wrong words next to each other – Joel thought he could see his name, but it was an accident of the way the words fell. That was all. The newspaper was old, he realised he had read these stories, these football scores, before. Over a week ago, in that pub, and he hadn't seen anything *then*. But maybe now... – he reached for the paper again...

What am I doing? he thought, why am I standing and reading a shit stained newspaper? Grimacing, he closed the bin and went back inside, where the crowd-sounds seemed quieter.

It had been the Saturday before. Whether the day's events were connected to what happened seemed unlikely at best, a forced connection from a later viewpoint. But it had seemed like the day when the pressure had changed.

Joel was on the Saturday shift. When he'd taken the job they hadn't mentioned anything about working weekends, but he was only a temp, and they could do what they wanted to him. He was fighting back yawns and a mild hangover when the boss called him into his office and told him he was fired.

"Wh.. what? But why?" Joel had said, too tired to be anything but perplexed.

"Listen, there isn't, I don't have to…" – his boss was a blustery, stuttering man, fat-lipped and heavily jawed. "I just have to call your agency, I don't have to give you a reason." The manager's words were all said in a brave little rush, and he was shifting his weight from one desk-job buttock to another. Joel realised that the man looked genuinely anxious about something.

Joel walked slowly back to his desk, to collect his things. None of his ex-colleagues looked at him, they were intent on their PCs – suddenly and mysteriously industrious. Joel started to speak to a girl with whom he thought he'd struck up a polite friendship, but she ignored him. In fact that wasn't quite true – she heard him and *tensed* at her PC – Joel could see the muscles tighten in her shoulders. But she carried on her impression of being a valued and eager employee.

Well, fuck 'em all, Joel thought as he dragged on his coat. He was better off out of here anyway – the agency would find him another job on Monday. What did he care what these people thought of him? He left without another word, his pockets full of office stationary.

The street outside was crowded with shoppers, so many of them it was as if Joel had got his seasons all wrong and it was really Christmas. Joel felt comforted by the crowd though, the sheer normality of it reset his emotional temperature after the strange and alienating way he had been treated. It was a fake solidarity, not conceived of or shared by the women struggling with pushchairs draped with carrier bags, or by the gang of youths all gathered heads together around one mobile phone, or by the beggar temporarily not seeking charity but just looking angry and baffled by those walking past. But it was a solidarity Joel felt none the less.

I'd still like to know *why*, he thought.

Someone crashed into him – well, it happens in crowds, Joel thought (he had been looking down, avoiding trash). But then the man gave a sarcastic, aggressive apology, and Joel looked up and saw the man was standing there as if daring him to make something of it. Had he crashed into him deliberately; was he drunk? The man wasn't large but there was something boorish in his looks – his little piglet eyes were glancing from side to side, as if seeking support from others before he did anything. Joel just walked away. The man hadn't smelt of booze, but now the thought had been put in his head Joel wanted a drink himself. The crowd seemed to be all moving in the opposite direction to him as he headed towards the nearest pub, making as many moves sideways as forwards. He heard whispers, some giggles. The quiet and dismal pub felt a blessed relief as he entered – the barman gave him a surly look but that was normal here. He got a beer and some food that he couldn't really afford. As he waited he picked up a newspaper to read. Same old shit, he saw, but he told himself that he couldn't be bothered with any real news after the morning he'd had. By the time his food came he'd read it twice, found nothing.

Why don't you call the police? Joel thought as he watched the people out front. They were committing trespass if nothing else; at least the ones at the front were, pushed over the boundary of the property by the ones at the back. And wasn't there a law against unlawful gatherings now, hadn't he read that? A story he should have read closely, but hadn't, for he'd felt no premonition... But Joel knew he wouldn't call the police – the idea was a sterile one in his mind, it didn't lead to explanation or closure; just a temporary moving on of the crowd. They would be dispersed, but still looking back towards Joel's house, still with that look in their eyes that Joel couldn't quantify; gleaming and feverish eyes turned back, promising...

That's it, he thought, looking down at them, it's like a fever, there's no cause, you can tell they're normal people really. And it will soon pass, stop spreading. How many of them were there now? His eyes got tired counting, and he lost which face he had started from. All the bodies outside his house looked too similar for him to be able to differentiate successfully, or to be able to keep Ian's cheap zombie DVDs from his mind. A chant started up – this time they got it going successfully. But Joel could hear no words, just gutturals to a *what-do-we-want-when-do-we-want-it* rhythm. It seemed to give them confidence, each gave their approval to each other's actions, and hence to their own.

Would the police even move them on, Joel thought, or just join in?

The sun was at its height – tracing its descent with his eyes he couldn't see the crowd leaving when it got dark. They would still be here, hours later, camouflaged and wolf-hungry in the dark, looking up at the light of the bedroom. Unless he did something. But what the hell was there to do?

Uncertain of his actions, Joel went downstairs, towards the front door.

The clatter of the previous Sunday's papers being delivered had stirred Joel's consciousness from its solipsistic hangover, like the sound held some promise of significance. Wearily, his eyes trudged across the familiar landscape of his broadsheet, the facts obscured to him by pages and pages of analysis, review, and 'Comment'. His headache was vicious – after getting the sack he'd felt he deserved to get drunk and now he felt nervous with heavy-lidded paranoia. He read through half the sections of the paper that he normally read, and when he looked up Ian was still on the sports pages of his paper. Joel's hangover was his excuse for wanting the tabloid, for he felt a child-like sense of self pity and irritation. Why didn't Ian hurry up and finish reading? His housemate was holding the paper in such a way that Joel couldn't see his face, just half a headline – CAUGHT ON CCTV! The rest was obscured.

"Hurry up with that," Joel said. "With that trash," he added.

"Did you know your face is in the newspaper?" Ian said.

"What?" Joel couldn't see the meaning of Ian's joke. "Fuck off."

"Look" – Ian refused to give him the paper, but showed him the offending page. The usual tabloid schlock, he saw, but off to one side of the 'news' (above an advert for an internet clairvoyant) was a thumb smudged photograph of Joel, close up and face on, like a passport photo or a mug-shot. The photo was a grainy black and white, and Joel couldn't see where or how it had been taken. It was outlined with a black frame, and captioned with his name and age (except they were a year out). Nothing about the photo had any relation to the rest of the page; but there it was.

"That's not me," Joel said pointlessly. "Is this some kind of joke?" He wasn't looking at Ian, but still staring at the newspaper page, waiting for something to click and make sense, like an optical illusion when you saw it the other way. He reached for the paper, wanting to take hold of it, to see if the mirage would fade at a closer distance, to be able to crumple the paper up with a laugh when he had seen the trick. But Ian moved it out of his reach.

"I'm *reading* that!"

"Ian, it's got my fucking photo in!" Joel said.

"So what? *I'm* reading it."

He must be in on it, Joel thought, taking a step back from his housemate. He couldn't have said why he felt agitated and threatened by seeing his face in the paper – after all, how did an obvious mistake at the printers actually affect his life? It was either an accident or a joke – there was no 'why' to it, no reason to intellectualise about it and expect any reward. But his mind was agitated and couldn't let it go – there must be some symbolism or causation he had missed. His hangover reminded him of its presence, and he winced and hung his head. Ian retreated back behind the paper, and Joel couldn't help but be suspicious. He went to make himself a coffee, figuring caffeine would be good for his nerves. He felt dislocated in the kitchen, because his mind was still thinking of the paper in the front room. Before the kettle had even half boiled he stormed back into the lounge. It had *his* picture in for fuck's sake!

"*Give* it to me," he said, but Ian was gone. He'd taken the newspaper with him.

Joel stood still for a second; he felt like something was going to happen, but nothing was. The kettle shrieked and silenced itself behind him. He told himself that nothing of significance had occurred, that his day was unchanged. He told himself that going up to Ian's room and demanding the paper would be childish and be admitting that it mattered. If this was a joke he was best off acting like he wasn't bothered. He went to make himself a black coffee and sat and read his own newspaper again, cover to cover. Everything he read seemed logical and realistic and quotidian, even the disasters and the remorseless wars, and none of it went any way to explaining why he still felt so sick and why his nerves had begun to clench at the slightest sound outside.

Joel paused in the act of unlocking the front-door, wondering if what he was about to do was wise. They were only people and he'd done nothing wrong. But again, he thought of newspapers naming and shaming, of gypsies handed round the country, of real petrol shortages caused by front-page lies about queues, of paediatricians beaten up by idiots who'd only half-read their idiot stories – he imagined the people who did such things looked exactly like the gaggle outside his house (he was looking through the spy-hole in the door): slack jawed and almost eager to be losing their identity, their arms hanging loosely for lack of action.

You're just being snobbish, he told himself, you don't even know that your photo appearing in that paper is the cause of all this. But he didn't see how it could be otherwise: they had printed his face two days in a row, and no doubt a third time today. What had they printed today – an explanation? As he looked out at the crowd he suspected the paper had printed something more prosaic – an address. They had done that for people on the child-crimes register, he remembered, until the police complained.

Joel straightened up from the spy-hole – he had to do *something*. The people outside were normal people and would listen to reason. He unlocked the door and flung it open; sunlight flooded in and he flinched like it was something unnatural, because he had been procrastinating in the ill-lit hall for so long. The people outside paused; words Joel had been unaware of died from their lips. Their eyes widened in unison; Joel tried to catch the gaze of a couple of them, but failed. He felt a curious lack of empathy, which he fought against. They didn't move.

"Hi," Joel said, wanting to sound normal; the words chocked in his throat and sounded weak. "Hello," he repeated. Someone shouted something at him, coarse and angry. Someone took a step towards him, as if to start a rush, but no momentum built up behind, and the man looked around at his fellows, confused and off balance. He was a young man, Joel's age, dressed in such a way that under different circumstances Joel would have assumed that their tastes were similar. The man swore at him, but the feeling that in a different world his words would have been friendly didn't leave Joel. The guy was *Ian's* age too, he thought. "Look, *what's going on?*" Joel said, his voice raised, speaking directly to the young man who had taken a step forward. The inane thought that they both had the same trainers clouded Joel's mind, and he shook his head. "What is going on?" he repeated.

The young man looked back at the the crowd, and then raised his fist at Joel and started shouting. It was no chant, and any rhythm was a by-product of his anger. His face was twisted and transformed, and Joel wasn't sure if his feeling of dislocation was because what he was seeing was unrealistic, or because what he had been expecting had been. His head swam as if processing two different sets of sensory impressions together – the words of the boy in the crowd recombined in forms he couldn't understand, a Doppler-effect between them.

"*Please* just tell me why..." Joel started to say in exasperation. The young man's face twisted in anger at his appeal, and he took another step towards him; this time a few of the others did too. They only need to get slightly more worked up, Joel thought, and they'll rush me. He half wished they would – then he could sue their asses off. But the feeling of potential violence unnerved him, and instead he shut the door. The last thing he saw was some of the crowd bending down, as if to pick up stones.

The kids had been shouting and swearing at everyone; it wasn't just him. Joel kept his head down as he walked. Monday – and he wasn't at work.

He had called the agency that morning but they had said there was no work, not with the downturn. It was the first time the employment agency had failed to find him an assignment – maybe he should sign up with another? But Joel felt a sense of fatalism, of lethargy – not that nothing mattered, but that what did matter wasn't here. Something had yet to begin. It was a stupid feeling, undeniable.

"Fuckin' layabout!" one of the kids called again, triggering giggles and expletives from his friends. "Fuckin' student!" – but, Joel realised, that last insult had come from a different angle, been in a deeper register. He looked up and saw workmen leering from some scaffolding, swearing and doing mincing impressions of him. Joel wanted to give them the finger, but didn't dare. He just carried on walking. He wasn't going anywhere, but he hadn't wanted to stay inside. He had been brooding in there, and he had thought that leaving the house would break the chain between what had happened yesterday and his current state of mind. But every time he tried to think of something else his errant thoughts found a way back home – *his picture had been in the newspaper and he didn't know why.*

Where had Ian gone yesterday? After he had disappeared with the paper Joel had stayed in all day but not seen him again. The waiting had stopped him doing anything, and been pointless for he hadn't known what he would say to Ian if he did see him; hadn't known why he wanted him to return. He had read his own paper a third time, and maybe it had been his mood but this time it seemed dumbed-down and tabloidesque: the way they crowed about the resignation of a Minister that they claimed to have predicted the day before; the self-fulfilling prophecy of the Fashion section, predicting next season's trends. When Joel had forced himself to bed, Ian hadn't been back; before Joel had risen Ian had presumably already left for work.

But you're being stupid, Joel thought. Ian's wasn't the only copy of that newspaper in the world. There were at least three newsagents within walking distance. He sped up, leaving the taunting kids behind, pleased that his walk now had some purpose. Maybe he would find that the other copies of yesterday's paper were normal, and that the whole thing had been a joke. He imagined some standard story of jingoism or whipped up paranoia in place of his mug-shot.

"Have you got any copies of yesterday's papers left?" he asked the teenager behind the counter at the nearest newsagent. The boy looked at him like he was an idiot, shook his head at him like he was deaf. Embarrassed, Joel bought a copy of that day's paper instead, aware that the lad was still staring at him. He tried to look normal. He didn't want the paper – he stood outside and flicked through the pages, ready to dump it into the bin as soon as he had checked its contents. The stories and photographs jerked from page to page like a faulty flick-book. It was enough to establish that the world and the paper's view of it hadn't changed: celebrity scandals that kept them celebrities, feel-good charity and knee-jerk editorials, stories of foreign disasters in which one British person had grazed their knee. Earthbound astrologers and money-off coupons. His face.

Joel almost dropped the paper. He stared at his own face staring back. It was a different shot, at a different angle, taken outside for there was a green blur for a backdrop (he had warranted colour this time). Again there was no context, no connection with the news stories on the page. But there was a longer caption this time: again Joel's name and age, but it also said CURRENTLY UNEMPLOYED.

"What the fuck?" Joel said out-loud; an old lady glared at him, her small dog yapped and glared at him too. She was still twittering and muttering to herself as she tied her dog to a lamppost and went into the newsagent. He glared back at the dog, disliking the way it had absorbed its owner's pre-war conservatism. The pet strained on its leash and looked as if it wanted to attack him, yapping its self-importance to the street. Joel didn't turn away but stood watching the little beast. Eventually its owner came back out the shop – is she still muttering about me? Joel thought.

She had a newspaper tucked under one arm – the same one he'd just bought.

Joel went back into the shop, not putting his new paranoia under scrutiny. He bought every copy of the newspaper that had printed his photo. Again, the boy behind the counter looked at him like he was crazy; Joel could barely carry them all up to the till. "I'm collecting the coupons," he said to the boy's look of tensed incredulity.

Later, at the recycling centre, he checked each copy before he threw it into the paper-bank. Not only for an absence of his face with real news in its place (although that would have been welcome) but, if his face had to be there then he was looking for an *explanation*. A paragraph misplaced from earlier editions, a sentence maybe, that would tell why he was considered newsworthy. He felt like even a comma in the right place would lead to clarification. But the papers were identical, and by the time he'd checked them all his hands were black with print.

CURRENTLY UNEMPLOYED he thought – how had they known? The agency had only told him they had no work this morning, otherwise he would have been in some office or warehouse as normal. But, Joel supposed that was the least of the mystery. He headed back home, weary, sweaty, his face smudged with ink where he had wiped away his perspiration. The builders took another break to do impressions of him; kids shouted and swore in his face then ran away giggling. He could no longer pretend that it wasn't directed towards him personally.

When he reached his front door it was dripping with smashed eggs – Halloween come early. Those fucking kids, he thought as he looked at the mess, shell and slime like some form of obscure and threatening graffiti; meaning warped as it slid downwards.

Ian's bedroom window faced the street, where the crowd gathered; Joel's room was at the back of the house, with a view of the small garden, more gravel than grass, surrounded by low, stone walls. Over the other side he could see other people's back gardens, and the alleys that led down the side of their houses to the front of their streets. Even from his back room, Joel could hear the crowd. It was still a small mob, the last he had looked, unsure of itself or its geography, and they had no presence on any other road.

Outside into the garden, Joel thought, over the wall and a quick sprint and he could escape and go – where? And to what purpose?

To find today's newspaper was one reason, he thought, to find out what those bastards have written about me today. For surely, whatever text accompanied his picture on this third day must be more substantial than merely his name and a misquoted age? Surely, to draw this crowd there must have been *allegations*, something factual that he could refute. Those people round the front of his house had to be there for a reason. It wasn't enough to think that the mere appearance of his face in the press could have caused this display of ill-feeling. No, it had to be that they thought he'd done something which they wouldn't; that he had something that they wanted.

He went to the other side of the house, to Ian's old room. The noise of the crowd was louder – the neighbours must be disturbed by it, Joel thought, why hadn't they complained? Why was this being allowed to continue?

All these questions are getting you nowhere, he thought.

But he still felt reluctant to actually do anything. After all, he'd first thought of escaping via the back garden hours ago – hopping over a low wall and running to an empty street was hardly a plan of genius – but he hadn't acted on it. Just like had been reluctant to call the police, his friends; even his family. Anything he did would be an admittance that this wasn't just going to blow over, that despite the unrealistic and other-worldly aspect that it had, it was all real enough.

He opened the window in Ian's room, and looked down at the people gathered outside his house. There was a pause in their chanting, they held up their arms to him – all Joel could see was a sea of clutching hands. The crowd cried out angrily, as if they had all just had the same thought. It was if they expected their cries to move him, their grasping hands to reach him, to draw him down into their embrace, to feel the full force of their anger. Joel leaned forward to get a better count of them. Maybe twenty five, thirty – it was impossible to be accurate. Something thrown slammed against the window pane, and Joel recoiled, but it was only an egg. Joel hastily shut the window again, for he didn't want to prompt a barrage, and as he did so he felt a strange feeling of both relief and disappointment. He imagined falling from that window, arms folded, into that waiting crowd. It would certainly be a way to end it.

And that was why he really hadn't called up his mates, or the police, or made a dash for it – because what if that didn't end it? What if his final card was played but the game carried on? He felt an edge of fear at the thought, the more fearful because he sensed it could become uncontrollable, sensed that his actions and emotions could become as irrational and senseless as those of the people surrounding his home.

It was just gone half past two – it was summertime. Joel told himself there were hours of daylight yet. There was no need to do anything straight away (although the thought of them still there, shouting and edging towards his door come darkness was not one that he wanted to think).

Joel left Ian's bedroom, walked along the landing towards his own room. There was the slam of something against the front window, and he turned automatically to look. Something about the view, and his nervous state, triggered a memory – Ian. Ian on the day he had left. Joel remembered the insults, the feeling that they had been teetering on the edge of irrational violence. And hadn't that been another change in pressure; looking back now didn't Ian's actions seem like the harbinger of what was to come, hadn't his personality then been a single-sized version of that of the crowd outside?

Joel decided that he *did* have to leave the house as soon as he could after all. Because there was no reason why Ian couldn't return, and Ian still had a key.

He had entered the house, not bothering to clean off the dripping egg behind him, and shut the doors on the shouts of the kids outside.

"Ian?" he had called. "Is anyone there?" – like he was one of those people who deserve to get got in horror movies. He had been unnerved by the silence of the house after the clamour of the street, and although he knew Ian obviously wasn't home it was hard not to tread quietly, to crane his neck at every imaginary sound.

Ian should be back from work by now, Joel thought some hours later. He didn't know when he had last even seen him – but yes he did, it had been Sunday morning, Ian's face hidden behind that tabloid with the CELEBRITY EXCLUSIVE! on the front cover. "Do you know your face is in the paper?"... that was pretty much the last he'd seen of him. It's ridiculous, Joel thought, where the hell is he? His housemate's disappearance just seemed one more stupid thing, after his sacking, after his mug-shot appearing in place of real news. The ambiguities seemed to be piling up. Joel felt that if he could just find out where Ian had gone, then it would at least take the edge off his other vague anxieties – prove right the voice that whispered that there was a reason for these things happening, just like there was for everything. Maybe, finding Ian would actually resolve some of the other mysteries too, like the neat and tidy ending of a well scripted film.

Besides, Joel thought, as he climbed the stairs towards Ian's bedroom, maybe he *is* in there, ill or hurt and I can help. He knew this thought was fantasy but it carried him up to the closed door.

The door to Ian's room was frosted glass, and Joel couldn't see anything but the light-shape of the front window as he peered in. He knocked, stupidly, leaving a pause so that Ian could reply and straighten things out, leaving the pause longer and longer until it got ridiculous and Joel had to admit that no one was in there. He knocked again, then opened the door, feeling a sense of transgression. As he pushed it open the door was blocked by something – Joel pushed harder, felt something move back. It was a cardboard box, with all Ian's CDs inside of it. It looked like it had been sealed shut with Sellotape, but it was coming unpeeled. The wardrobe door swung open as Joel entered, like a mouth hanging gaping and empty; the coat-hangers were bare and shirts and suits were thrown all over the bed. Is he going away? Joel thought – it looked more like he was moving out.

The wastepaper bin was overflowing – not knowing why, Joel moved over. Bare floorboards betrayed him to the empty house. He picked the contents out of the litter bin – the surprise he felt was automatic, conditioned behaviour. Deep down he wasn't surprised by what he had picked up: newspaper, tabloid. Each double page had been separated and screwed up into a ball; Joel unfolded them all, seeing how the stories from the front of the paper segued into those from the back. Anyone would think that there was an election on by the attacks at "woolly liberals"; anyone would think there was a war on by the paranoid insistence to close the borders. All spilling into gurning celebrity endorsements, and feel-good sporting jingoism. Joel found the page with his face on, and unfolded and smoothed it out as best he could. Someone had viciously and comprehensively scribbled his eyes and mouth out with black pen.

He heard a noise downstairs, and he would have had chance to get away but he had been deep in thought, and the sound of the door chimed with his thoughts because despite the time of day it sounded like a newspaper being delivered – an addendum maybe, a recall and retraction. So he stood up slowly, didn't think to disguise his footsteps as he walked across the wooden floor of Ian's bedroom. He practically crashed into his housemate in the doorway, almost chest to chest. He had probably never been so physically close to Ian; certainly he had never realised how tall he was before.

"What the *fuck*," Ian said, "are you doing in my bedroom?" Looking back, Joel realised Ian had been angry already, somehow, there had been no escalation of the argument because it was like they had been pitched forward ten minutes into the crux of it; as if Joel had missed the intervening sections, the exposition.

"Look, Ian, I was just..." Joel said, but his words lacked strength and he had no ready explanation to hand. Ian was like some violent force gathering in the doorway. "What the fuck..." he started to repeat, but stopped and shoved Joel instead. Joel was off balance and almost fell over the box of CDs behind him. He had been ready for an argument, not a fight, and he felt sick with sudden fear. But there was no sense that this was unexpected, not in the sense that it didn't follow naturally from what had happened before. It made no sense but he thought of a triangle inevitably gathering to a point. Joel regained his balance, backed away, hands raised.

"Now *look!*" he said. "I heard... a, a noise. I came in to see what... it must have been a draught..." Ian shoved him again. Joel did fall this time, striking his head against the bed with such force he couldn't hear properly. Ian was shouting, advancing. Joel scrambled to his feet, aware that there was not much further space he could back into. Was his head really ringing? He could hear the *noise* of Ian's shouting, just not the actual words. He shook his head, and the sounds came slightly back into focus.

But Ian had reverted to asking him what the fuck he thought he was doing in his room.

"This is ridiculous!" Joel shouted, suddenly angry at this further stupidity, this further mess that he didn't need. "I'm sorry if I came into your room, alright, but this is..." His thoughts changed tack: "Why are you *packing*? Are you moving out?"

Ian hit him, swearing something as he did so.

Joel fell over again, hands clutched to his face where he had been punched – his split lip dribbled blood over his chin. He landed in among the sheets of newspaper that he had flattened out, as if ready-placed to absorb his bleeding.

"I ought to make you eat that fuckin' newspaper!" Ian shouted. "I ought to make you choke on it!" There seemed to be some sense in his words that this would have been a *fitting* punishment, as if it would have satisfied some crude and demotic symbolism. But at that point Joel was more worried that Ian would make his threats true than clarifying what they meant. He could imagine the taste of ink, the taste of the balls of newspaper that Ian had rolled up again being fed one after another down his throat, ticklish and denying him breath. Imagined too Ian hitting him again and again, as if to scribble out his features just as he'd scribbled them out on the page.

Joel looked up, but thankfully Ian was still where he had been. His housemate looked behind him, as if there was someone there, but naturally there wasn't. His temper didn't seem to diminish but became more uncertain somehow, less sure of itself. He wasn't as big as he had seemed – Joel watched as Ian went back to the doorway, held the door open for him.

"Get out," he said, his mouth tight with distaste as he looked down at Joel sprawled on the floor.

"But," Joel said, "Ian, why are you...?"

"Get out! Get out you fuckin' freak!" – fearing another outbreak of violence, worse this time, more fearsome and irredeemable, Joel scuttled to his own bedroom, shut the door behind. He stood there, still and tensed, ear against the frosted glass of his own door. He heard the muffled sound of Ian carrying his things downstairs, struggling with the boxes and suitcases on the stairs. Joel was scared that Ian would come for him again, but half wanted him to as well. He found that he was shaking with an anger whose strength surprised him, a kind of anger he had felt rational, well-rounded people didn't feel. He half-wished that Ian would try to come into his room so that he could stand up and demand to know what the hell was going on; and to punch the fucker if he was accused of being a whiny liberal again. But he still shrank every time it sounded like footsteps were heading his way.

Eventually he heard the front-door open and shut; no sound of keys being pushed through the letterbox though. Maybe Ian wasn't really moving out for good? Not that he cared – let the fucker go, Joel thought, he could manage the rent on his own. Quite how, without a job, was a thought that could wait for a cooler and more rational day. Cautiously, he went downstairs and found everything alcoholic that might help him sleep. Then he crept back up to his room and tried to calm his nerves. He tried to text some friends three times, but gave up – he couldn't express how he felt in abbreviations and text-speak. And besides, what if his mates replied with scorn, and it was his expectation of anything otherwise that was unworldly, naïve? Ian's seen that paper, he thought, they've all seen the paper. He didn't know why that thought felt important, because it was just a picture, a mistake of a picture at that. But he didn't call them.

Instead he got drunk on his own, and watched zombie films, and couldn't sleep.

Outside, next morning, was a crowd.

~

Joel took a final look at the people outside his house – in full view in the top window his appearance caused a ripple of movement, a braying and confused sound that could have been words. But little more than that – unless I actually throw myself to the wolves I'm quite safe, Joel thought. They're quite witless at the moment. But that could all change if Ian returned, he could be the catalyst they needed. Joel had made up his mind to leave the house. But he had wanted to take one last look at the crowd to try and determine the common denominator in all those upturned and slack-jawed faces – what made *these* people want to come and rant outside his house? But there was no similarity that he could distinguish – the clouds made the light bad and smudged people's features; to Joel they looked non-descript, men and women so generic he could picture them in any job, being in any alignment or relationship.

Mentally shrugging, trying to shake off his failure (and he knew it was a failure) Joel turned and walked out of Ian's room. He went across the landing and into his own room, and over to the wardrobe, trying to find clothes with which to disguise himself from people who had only ever seen photographs of his face.

The escape from his own house went much as he'd pictured. He went out into the back garden, glad it was sealed off and invisible to the street – was it his imagination or did they sound more restless and volatile out front, more violent even? Then a scramble over his back wall and into the garden beyond. I am a criminal now, Joel thought vaguely; trespass. The garden he was in was an unkempt patch of grass, upon which a group of electrical goods were leaking old oil. The sound of the mob already seemed fainter, impotent, less pressing on the ear than the territorial call of a house sparrow eyeing him watchfully. Joel lurched into an unhurried jog round the side of the dull brick house, and out into the main road.

Immediately he saw two people running, past him, round the corner which Joel had cut by his vault over the wall. They ignored him in their single-minded race towards his house. The look on their faces made Joel's new confidence quaver – he hadn't realised how close to violence these people were. He walked in the opposite direction as quickly as he could. What could these people possibly be accusing him of? Yet he felt no anger, but an obscure guilt, as he remembered the petty wrongs of his life: the girls lied to, the friends let slip, the usual moments of apathy, snobbery, or dogmatism. What was in that fucking newspaper? his thoughts repeated without their previous incredulity. Where had they begun?

As he entered the newsagent he felt his disguise flimsy – as if an ill-fitting coat and woollen hat could disguise who he was, or hide the red flush that wouldn't leave his face! His anxiety was increased because the shop was crowded with people who were all muttering. He tried to listen but couldn't tell if the euphemisms and veiled threats were directed at him or one of the usual press targets:

"The police?" a man was saying "What use are the police, their hands are tied. *We* need to sort them out, that's what..." – a 'they', Joel thought, I've never been part of a 'they'. But:

"It's disgusting," a woman was saying, "jail's too good for the likes of him, they should bring back hanging, they really should..." – singular, Joel thought, so maybe they *are* talking about me.

Why were there so many people in the shop anyway? He tried to blank out their words, and turned to the newspapers to look for the one which had printed his face. But, Joel though, how did he know it had only been one? The crowd's words continued to accuse him; all the magazines and papers half-revealed his crimes, yet when he took them from the shelf it was to reveal the banal drug addictions of super-models, the predilections of celebrity-adulterers, and the over-enthusiastic castigation of those who had fallen from tabloid grace.

Joel was pulling the titles from the shelves in no order now, not able to find the one whose publication of his face had started all of this. People were looking at him – he forced himself to calm down. When he found the paper, he flicked through it in the shop: topless celebrities on a beach, disputed casualty figures, new diet fads. He knew none of the pictures were of him; but it was hard to tell, with the smudged and grainy CCTV stills, the over-exposed and oddly-angled paparazzi shots. He tried to take it slow – headlines and stories kept catching his eye before he realised that no, they weren't *his* crimes or misdemeanours. In many cases punishment had already been served and the tone of the paper was smirking, self-satisfied. Joel felt that when he found the right story, *his* story, all the others would make a new and deserved kind of sense too...

He was barely half way through the paper when someone pushed him. Taken by surprise, Joel staggered; the newspaper fluttered from his hand. Distressed, he turned round to face the man who had pushed him – was it the same drunk who'd accosted him in the street on the day of his sacking? Joel wasn't sure – the boorish, over-defined face seemed to be the same, but not the man's almost preening air of self-confidence – he was a man who smiled and spoke with the knowledge that he had the backing of a full majority.

"*You*," he said. "I knew it was you!" And he shouted out to the people in the shop, drawing their attention...

People looked round, turned – I have to leave here, Joel thought. He moved towards the way out, not turning away from the man he faced. His back-stepping was stopped by the presence of someone behind – they had encircled him. He whirled away, felt hands pass by reaching out to grab him. They were forcing him back up another aisle, away from the exit! He kept walking with his back to them, and they kept walked slowly forward, moving him towards the back of the shop. Up close, he could barely focus on their faces; they were babbling and shouting but he couldn't understand. It was like being hemmed in by a different species; how would they react if he turned and ran? He didn't know but did so anyway, down the left-hand aisle. He saw a door marked with pictorials of fire and people fleeing – he barged though and heard the alarm of the shop scream like something denied behind him. He put his head down and ran, turning left, then left again...

He lost his pursuers (he could hear them behind him, but didn't turn around to see), but stayed near the newsagent – the thought of the paper he had dropped half-read kept him circling like an animal round a dangerous source of food. Today, surely, they'd printed the story that made sense of all this, the sentence that spelt out why... But he couldn't get to it! So he skulked around the shop, in the park opposite it, collar upturned in the streets alongside it, but never daring to go back in. Eventually, he saw them lock up, and darkness fell. He knew he couldn't go back to his house, and so he kept near the locked shop, not quite psyching himself up for a break-in. He peered at it from over the brick wall of the park, squatting uncomfortably in the damp grass. He thought vaguely that this wasn't his life, that really he was sitting at home watching TV, loathing work. But the thought was weak and all words – no images. He couldn't picture his parallel life; maybe it had never happened.

He didn't sleep, and so when in the dark early morning a van pulled up outside the shop, it still felt like it was the day before.

Two men got out of the van, and looked around, peered through the windows of the shop, banged on the door. One of them cursed and looked at his watch, the other shrugged and started taking tied up bundles of newspapers from the back of the van and leaving them on the pavement. Hot off the presses; Joel could practically smell them. Another car pulled up, and a flustered looking man got out, already talking. The first two men shook their heads, gestured at the parcels of newspapers on the street, and got back in the van. The third man swore half-heartedly at the van as it pulled off, then went and unlocked the shop's front door. Struggling, he picked up one of the bundles of newspapers and carried it slowly into the shop. He was gone a number of minutes before he returned for the next one, and Joel held his breath as he watched from over the wall. By the time he came back a third time the man looked tired, and already had a fag on the go. He slowly took another bundle of papers inside, and when he was out of sight in the shop Joel leapt over the wall of the park, ran across the street, and tried to pull a paper from the remaining pile. He knew it didn't matter which title it was anymore, they were all the same. The papers were tightly bound together with some kind of plastic strips, and Joel felt scared in case the third man came back out of the newsagent and caught him in his act of transgression. He managed to worm one of the papers free, and he started to sprint back towards the park again, but the noise of a large group of people deterred him – probably just drunk lads coming home late, he told himself, but better not to find out. Instead he ran down the side of the shop, and turned round the back of it – there were two commercial skips there, filled to overflowing with old newspapers, sheets of which were scattered and trod into the pavement of this small space. Some were banded up neatly, as if yesterday's news could be sold two for one; some were yellowed and fluttered sickly on the ground. Joel hunched down between the two large skips, ignoring the uncomfortable press of the metal against his back. It was still pre-dawn, still the previous night really, but there was just enough light to read the newspaper he had stolen. The date on the top of each page gave him an odd little feeling of excitement, like he was reading about future events before they had actually happened.

The first page obviously wasn't the one he wanted, for the story was a lurid and sensationalist murder – as far as Joel could make out someone had been practically torn apart with no rhyme or reason. All the usual tabloid condemnations were offered: MONSTERS, MOB JUSTICE – but Joel felt these words were so clichéd as to be half-hearted, as if they didn't really believe in the strong language they were using. Between the lines was a distinct excitement, heightened by the photograph which took up almost two thirds of the page – a non-descript, day-lit crime scene that could have been anywhere – some back alley somewhere.

But he was wasting time – Joel skimmed through the paper looking for his likeness; for the why and wherefore of his crimes that justified his picture being printed and the mob at his door. He couldn't see anything; he felt a curious mixture of relief and disappointment. Maybe it had finished, maybe the press had given up on whatever its little moral crusade had been, maybe his face would appear no more. But it was hard to believe, for there had yet to be an explanation; skipping the lurid front-page Joel started to read the paper more carefully, just to make sure.

The sun was starting to rise, but it wasn't getting lighter – Joel didn't sense the shadows that fell across him as he read, still looking for his answer. He was reading the paper in a 'corridor' between the two large skips (each taller than he was) and the brick wall of the newsagent. At the front of this corridor the people approached silently and waited as their numbers slowly built up.

Eventually, Joel was alerted and turned his head – the crowd blocked the way out, blurred and monstrous in his vision. He looked the other way – at the end of his corridor the wall of the shop took a right-angle, blocking him off. He scrambled to his feet, but there was nowhere to go.

He looked at the crowd's faces, at their tensed postures, and it was like Ian catching him in the act of trespass again: the way that they stood in the 'doorway' and blocked his escape, the feeling that if he tried to shove his way through then the violence simmering in their thoughts would become a reality. But the sheer number of them made it different too, the way the crowd seemed one body with one will, unconcerned with any petty doubts of its individual members. Ian had been uncertain of his right to inflict violence; the crowd felt no such ambiguity.

Were these the same people who'd been outside his house, or different? They didn't make a move yet, and more people arrived and started pushing at the back. *None of this is fair!* Joel thought; *just why me?* He tried to talk to them, but he didn't know what to say other than this obviously couldn't be happening, that he was in the wrong place, or wrong time. He paced back and forth in his trap, feeling condemned. They were shadow shapes of human beings, grunting incomprehensibly – but they were normal looking people at the same time, hugging themselves or stamping their feet to keep themselves warm in the early morning chill. Joel continued to try to talk to them, started to shout at them, but they didn't seem to understand, and the noise made them displeased, and they responded in words of their own that Joel couldn't comprehend.

The crowd continued to grow, the ones at the back who couldn't see pushing forwards so that those at the front were forced forward into the corridor – Joel looked into their faces and saw they were still reluctant to be the ones who actually started it, but they kept getting pushed further and further and so lent further legitimacy to what was going to happen. Joel was still shouting at them, no longer begging an explanation, but just to be let go. He saw nothing new in their faces, just the same myopic righteousness. A man was pushed to the front of the crowd – it looked like the drunk before, or like Ian, but Joel realised that the similarity was just his mind's final attempt to find order in what was happening. The man had been shoved into Joel, and he pushed him to get some room; Joel nearly slipped on the ripped sheets of newspaper underfoot. Someone else moved up alongside the man, was pressed forward right against Joel, pulling at Joel's ill-fitting coat to keep herself from falling over. He instinctively pushed her away, but more of the crowd were already pressing in behind her and she had nowhere to go. She pushed him backwards; his shoulder slammed against the metal skip, and he slipped. Trying to regain his feet, he reached out for something to keep himself upright; but his hand only found the body of someone else who was off balance because they were being pushed from behind, and this person shoved him away so that his head banged against the brick wall, and he fell. People moved forward so that they were practically standing on him; he covered his head with his arms on the floor. He knew that he was screaming, and that his screams sounded incomprehensible. Legs brushed against him, softly, then stumbled against him, then kicked him. There was another kick, and then another, either side of him now; hands reached to haul him up only to cast him down again. He heard the shout of the people at the back of the crowd, impatient to push forward for their share. He tasted blood, the taste sharp behind his closed eyes. More blows, one slamming into his head and simultaneously slamming it into the brick wall. Joel wished he could lose consciousness, for his terrified thoughts were useless, there was no way to stop what was happening, for it had already occurred. He opened his eyes one last time, saw the dark shapes looming over him, but saw too how the sunlight lit up the corridor he was trapped in, made its dimensions and appearance familiar – it looked like some back alley, that could have been anywhere...

He had been wrong to flick forward, he realised.

He was front-page news, after all.

JAMES EVERINGTON

EPILOGUE:
A DREAM ABOUT ROBERT AICKMAN

Last night, I dreamt I was in a bookshop. All the books were on rotating carousels; they were square and very thin with covers seemingly made of canvas or some sort of woven fabric. They only displayed the author's name on the front, not any titles, and to tell who the book was by you had to run your fingers over the embossed writing like Braille.

I was turning the carousel looking through the books and I wondered why there weren't any by Robert Aickman. As soon as I thought this, the carousel (which turned of its own accord) presented a book to me; I traced Aickman's name on the cover and then opened it.

All the pages were folded into each like the leaves of a map, but a thousand times more complicated and intricately layered. As I unfolded more and more pages I held them up to the light, and the paper was tough but almost see through, like an insect's wing. Each page spawned more and more pages. The next might have writing in all the alphabets of the world, or diagrams that drew themselves, or colourful illustrations like the Book Of Kells, or brand new periodic tables, or anatomical drawings of imaginary creatures.

~

I looked around the bookshop, and all the other people there had similar books open, their open pages unfolding and connecting like paper streamers between us. Everyone was smiling and everyone was reading, and I knew I'd never be able to shut the book that was opening and opening in my hands.

AUTHOR NOTES

Here are some notes on the stories, for those that want them. Those of you who'd prefer to avert their eyes, I won't be offended – I'll thank you for reading this far and let you get on with your lives.

Everyone else, here we go...

Falling Over

This story was originally written for *Penny Dreadnought* – a loose collective consisting of myself, Alan Ryker, Iain Rowan, and Aaron Polson, who occasionally publish themed anthologies of weird fiction. *Falling Over* was in the second volume called *Descartes' Demon* – an anthology of horror stories on the theme of 'epistemic doubt'.

'Epistemic' just means how we know things, and really there's only one way – through our senses. Which can deceive us. Or be deceived. Scary, no? And fertile soil from which to grow horror stories. Implicitly or explicitly, I think a lot of the best weird fiction is about doubt and about the paranoia that doubt can turn into. A lot of mine are, anyway.

Oh and I've *always* wanted to write a 'pod-people' story, despite the fact that like the central character in this story I've never actually read *The Body Snatchers*.

There's a lot of falling imagery in the stories in this book, so that's why I picked the title of this one as the overall title for the collection.

Fate, Destiny, And A Fat Man From Arkansas

This is the oldest story in the collection, and I guess the most straight-forward horror story here. There's a smidgen of Lovecraft, bolted onto the age-old idea of trespassers being punished… The horror that underpins it all however is the idea of being trapped in a series of events that can't be stopped; of being dragged to an unenviable end despite foreknowledge and one's own wishes…

I've no idea where the idea of having the fat man come from Arkansas came from; I think I just like the sound of the word.

Haunted

This was originally written for the first anthology published by *Cruentus Libri Press*, the premise for which was beautifully simple. Called *100 Horrors*, the book was to feature one hundred horror authors each with a horror story one hundred words long or less.

My contribution was *Haunted* and, if you count the title, it is *exactly* one hundred words long. Yes, I am a show off.

And yes, the main character is called Eleanor in homage to the greatest haunted house story of them all…

New Boy

Another falling story…

I used to work in a building very much like the one described in this story, although obviously the tale itself is complete fiction. I worked on the tenth floor and had a desk next to the windows, from where I could see the city. I spent a lot of time bored and staring out at the view but nothing as exciting as seeing a person fall past ever happened. However a bad job with a good view is a spur to the imagination, and sometime during that period the idea for this story came to me.

The Time Of Their Lives
The idea for this one came whilst reading the story *The Break* by Terry Lamsley – from the first few pages I was trying guess where the story was going. I didn't guess correctly at all (Lamsley is too good a writer for that) but *The Time Of Their Lives* grew from one of those wide of the mark guesses. It took on its own life so that in the end it doesn't share much with *The Break* apart from being set in a somewhat odd hotel and having a young protagonist. Bizarrely, when I came to edit it for this collection, it reminded me of Roald Dahl's *The Witches* more than anything else.

I was on holiday in the Cotswolds at the time, so that's why the story is set there. It's a truly lovely part of the world – and as a horror writer I take that as a *challenge*.

The Man Dogs Hated
A slightly baffling one this, I admit, even to me. The words came to me, and I wrote them down, and tidied up the sentence structure and other boring things where it was needed. Sometimes your only conscious involvement in it all seems to be just getting the thing fixed on paper before the words fade. Oh I could tell you it's a story about conformity and the theme of the scapegoat, but that's only because I've *read* it a few times, not because I wrote it.

I quite like dogs, but I'm a cat person myself.

Sick Leave

Quite obviously, this is about the fear of death. More specifically, how we turn a blind eye to our upcoming deaths; how we readily speculate about what good things might happen to us in the future but hardly ever about the one bad thing that is *definitely* going to happen to us.

I've noticed before that children sometimes seem, from our adult perspective, morbidly interested in death. As if they, unlike us, still haven't *quite* got their heads round it and managed to put it from their minds.

Drones

This was written for *The Sirens Call* magazine, who were looking for stories based on the theme of 'horror from the point of view of the observer'.

The observer – that's interesting, I thought, but I haven't got any stories that fit right now, and the deadline is in a few days so I haven't time to come up with anything... Ah well.

Around this time I'd also been turning over a vague idea in my head about a story featuring a soldier in a modern day war, who did little but stare at computer screens all day like any other office worker. And about what he might see on those screens that wasn't strictly speaking there. Now you'd think my conscious mind would have been smart enough to think: *Computer screens? From the point of view of the observer? There's a connection there...!* but no. But my subconscious, which is obviously the brains of the outfit, must have made the connection overnight, for the next morning I awoke with this in my head.

Not just the idea for *Drones* mind you, but the whole shebang: the plot, the lead character's voice, the first lines, the last lines...

This has happened to me only occasionally; when it does the story seems very fragile, like a soap bubble, and I know I have to get it written down as quickly as I can before it bursts. So I went straight downstairs, boiled the kettle, and wrote the first draft in a couple of hours.

The next day I attempted to decipher my cramped and frantic handwriting, and wrote out a second draft; the day after that it was typed up and sent off to the good folks at *The Sirens Call* who accepted it, bless them.

Public Interest Story

The British tabloid press are a national fucking disgrace. Small-minded, bigoted deceivers; phone-hacking, police-bribing, corrupt bastards, blatantly serving the interests of the rich and amoral whilst pretending to speak for the public.

And we lap it up.

The original version of this story was written before the *News Of The World* phone hacking scandal came to light. If it had been a too literal a tale of press persecution I probably would have had to bin it when that story broke, because there's no way my imagination could have outdone the actual reality of how the Murdoch press operated.

Fortunately my take on tabloid scaremongering is a more Kafkaesque, surreal trip into modern day damnation, so I still think it holds up – although who knows what press scandals and corruption unknown to me now will have been uncovered by the time you are reading this?

As well as the tabloid angle, this is also a story about crowds of course, about mob-rule. Out of all of my stories it's probably the one that scares *me* the most. Human beings are the scariest monsters of course, and something about the idea of being trampled to death by a group of people so far gone into group-think that I can't even reason with them anymore scares the hell out of me.

Epilogue: A Dream About Robert Aickman

This one came to me exactly as the title suggests: in a dream. Events are exactly as they occurred in that dream, to the best of my waking knowledge.

It seemed a suitable note to end on, for what is writing for if not the sharing of dreams?

You can find out more about my other books and general goings on at www.jameseverington.blogspot.co.uk/

MORE FROM INFINITY PLUS

Ghostwriting
by Eric Brown
www.infinityplus.co.uk/books/eb/ghostwriting.htm

Over the course of a career spanning twenty five years, Eric Brown has written just a handful of horror and ghost stories – and all of them are collected here.

They range from the gentle, psychological chiller "The House" to the more overtly fantastical horror of "Li Ketsuwan", from the contemporary science fiction of "The Memory of Joy" to the almost-mainstream of "The Man Who Never Read Novels". What they have in common is a concern for character and gripping story-telling.

Ghostwriting is Eric Brown at his humane and compelling best.

"Brown is a terrific storyteller as the present collection effectively proves... All in all an excellent collection of entertaining and well written dark fiction." —*Hellnotes*

"Eric Brown joins the ranks of Graham Joyce, Christopher Priest and Robert Holdstock as a master fabulist" —Paul di Filippo

**For full details of infinity plus books
see www.infinityplus.co.uk/books**

One Of Us
by Iain Rowan
www.infinityplus.co.uk/books/ir/oneofus.htm

Anna is one of the invisible people. She fled her own country when the police murdered her brother and her father, and now she serves your food, cleans your table, changes your bed, and keeps the secrets of her past well hidden.

When she used her medical school experience to treat a man with a gunshot wound, Anna thought it would be a way to a better life. Instead, it leads to a world of people trafficking, prostitution, murder and the biggest decision of Anna's life: how much is she prepared to give up to be one of us?

Shortlisted for the UK Crime Writers' Association Debut Dagger award, *One of Us* is a novel by award-winning writer Iain Rowan.

Praise for Iain Rowan's *Nowhere To Go*:

"Fine examples of modern crime stories, gripping and perceptive, probing the dark secrets of the human soul, just like an old Alfred Hitchcock movie... Crime enthusiasts must not miss the book: this is noir at its very best." —*SF Site* featured review

"A short story writer of the highest calibre." —Allan Guthrie, winner of Theakston's Crime Novel of the Year

"Every story in this collection is a gem... classy and clever Brit Grit at its best." —Paul D Brazill at *Death By Killing*

**For full details of infinity plus books
see www.infinityplus.co.uk/books**

Genetopia
by Keith Brooke
www.infinityplus.co.uk/books/kb/genetopia.htm

Searching for his missing sister, Flint encounters a world where illness is to be feared, where genes mutate and migrate between species through plague and fever. This is the story of the struggles between those who want to defend their heritage and those who choose to embrace the new.

"A minor masterpiece that should usher Brooke at last into the recognized front ranks of SF writers" —*Locus*

"I am so here! *Genetopia* is a meditation on identity – what it means to be human and what it means to be you – and the necessity of change. It's also one heck of an adventure story. Snatch it up!" —Michael Swanwick, Hugo award-winning author of *Bones of the Earth*

"Keith Brooke's *Genetopia* is a biotech fever dream. In mood it recalls Brian Aldis's *Hothouse*, but is a projection of twenty-first century fears and longings into an exotic far future where the meaning of humanity is overwhelmed by change. Masterfully written, this is a parable of difference that demands to be read, and read again." —Stephen Baxter, Philip K Dick award-winning author of *Evolution* and *Transcendent*

**For full details of infinity plus books
see www.infinityplus.co.uk/books**

The Fabulous Beast
by Garry Kilworth
www.infinityplus.co.uk/books/gk/fabulousbeast.htm

A set of beautifully crafted tales of the imagination by a writer who was smitten by the magic of the speculative short story at the age of twelve and has remained under its spell ever since.

These few stories cover three closely related sub-genres: science fiction, fantasy and horror. In the White Garden murders are taking place nightly, but who is leaving the deep foot-prints in the flower beds? Twelve men are locked in the jury room, but thirteen emerge after their deliberations are over. In a call centre serving several worlds, the staff are less than helpful when things go wrong with a body-change holiday.

Three of the stories form a set piece under the sub-sub-genre title of 'Anglo-Saxon Tales'. This trilogy takes the reader back to a time when strange gods ruled the lives of men and elves were invisible creatures who caused mayhem among mortals.

Garry Kilworth has created a set of stories that lift readers out of their ordinary lives and place them in situations of nightmare and wonder, or out among far distant suns. Come inside and meet vampires, dragons, ghosts, aliens, weremen, people who walk on water, clones, ghouls and marvellous wolves with the secret of life written beneath their eyelids.

"Kilworth's stories are delightfully nuanced and carefully wrought.' —*Publishers Weekly*

"A bony-handed clutch of short stories, addictive and hallucinatory." —*The Times*

"Here is a writer determined and well equipped to contribute to the shudder-count." —*The Guardian*

For full details of infinity plus books
see www.infinityplus.co.uk/books

Printed in Great Britain
by Amazon